PAGE OF SWORDS

AINSLEY BOOTH

SADIE HALLER

COPYRIGHT

ABOUT PAGE OF SWORDS

Bas:

Meadow is off-limits. She's my tenant, my friend, and most importantly, a woman who has her shit together when I famously do not.

But in the dark of night, when the filthiest of fantasies take over, it's her soft, curvy body I'm tying up, holding down, and dominating.

So I throw myself into yet another new project—a Halloween street party. It's supposed to be clean and wholesome, but with each planning session, a little bit of kink slides in. And my depravity is just twisted enough that I start to imagine the good doctor is enjoying the double entendres.

Meadow:

I've been keeping a secret from Bas since the moment I met him, and everything that's happened since then—our friendship, my inappropriate crush, the fact that I moved into the apartment over his bar—is tainted by that lie.

I need to confess everything, and I will, after Halloween. Because there's no way I'm going to miss the hottest party of the year—or lose what might be my only chance to explore the hidden side of my desires I've never been brave enough to let loose before.

THE HALLOWEEN STREET PARTY RULES:

- No nudity. Leave your undies on when you climb onto the spanking bench!
- Adults only, please. The entire street is licensed for liquor and inappropriate language.
- Whatever you do, don't fall in love with your best friend. The costumes aren't real, and the feelings are fragile.

MEADOW

EVERY SO OFTEN I forget where I am, who I am, and what's appropriate to say at work. This is the only excuse I have for what I say in a moment of exhausted, unvarnished honesty at the end of an interdepartmental meeting, when the surgeon chairing it says something about having to plan around maternity leave. And then casts a judgemental eye in my direction.

"I'd have to have sex in order to get knocked up, so we're safe there."

In my defence, it's under my breath, and the only person who really hears the whole thing is Max Donovan, a paediatrician with a decent sense of humour.

He manages to contain his chuckle behind a subtle smirk, and although the general surgeon across boardroom table gives me a weird look, the meeting wraps up and everyone hustles off to their morning rounds or into the OR for the first procedures of the day.

I have the day off, so I stay seated and try not to look mortified when Max lingers, too.

Once we're alone, he laughs out loud.

"Shut up, you're happily taking care of your wife all the time, aren't you?"

He winks. "That's between me and Violet."

"That's a yes, and I hate you both." I groan. "I can't believe I said that out loud."

"You're exhausted." Now the look he gives me is pure concern, and I get it. We were both on call last night, and I had a difficult surgery in the middle of the night, repairing a bad haemorrhage in a new mom. Max was on hand for the birth, and made sure to come back after my patient woke up again to reassure her that her baby was just fine.

That was my third rough shift in a row. "I thought once I was done with residency, my life would return to normal. Somewhat."

He shakes his head. "That's a lie we tell new trainees to get them into the cult."

"Accurate." I sigh and roll my neck. "Okay, I'm going to the gym to work out my frustration—shut up again—and then I'm going home to sleep like the dead."

He rubs his jaw. "I, uh, have a timely confession to make."

"What?"

"I talked you up to a friend of mine—no names, just a general description—a few weeks ago. He asked for your number, and I said I'd give his to you if you might be interested."

On the one hand, a blind date is the worst thing in the world.

On the other…I haven't had sex in six months, and good sex in more than a year. Fuck it. Even though I know how this is going to go down, I'm game. "Gimme."

"You don't want to know anything about him?"

"Is he a serial killer?"

"No."

"Misogynist?"

"He does his best not to be." Max clears his throat when I give him a side-eye at that. "No. He's pretty cool. He owns a bar in

Metcalfe, but he's always got something new on the go. A creative type."

"Is that code for he works random hours and understands the life of an obstetrician?"

Max grins. "Something like that."

"Gimme gimme."

I GO home and crawl into bed, but when I wake up, my first thought is this guy. Sebastian, Max wrote down on a card. *"But everyone calls him Bas."* Good to know. Bas the bartender.

So I get up, have a shower, and drive into the country because who am I kidding?

If Max thinks this guy might be for me, I'm intrigued.

Metcalfe is an adorable hamlet, little more than a set of intersections. Sebastian's bar, Duke & Main, is in fact at the intersection of Duke Street and Main Street.

How hipster.

And yet it works. The façade is real rustic, not hipster-out-of-the-box, and there's an amazing looking coffee shop across the street. *Tessa*, it says in the window. *Coffeebar and Bakery* is written under the flowing name, all of it in a delicate script.

I stop there first, because coffee is courage.

There's a tall brunette woman behind the counter who gives me a welcoming smile. "What can I get for you?"

"I'll take a short espresso shot, please," I say as I peruse the baked goods in the glass display. I want a muffin, but it's probably rude to bring food to a blind-date ambush.

If it doesn't go well, I'll come back.

Who am I kidding? I'll be back either way. "Just the shot for now."

The big espresso machine behind the counter hisses to life and I turn around, peering out the window at Duke & Main.

"What brings you to Metcalfe?" the barista asks.

The real answer would be way oversharing. "I had the afternoon off and wanted to come for a drive," I say absentmindedly.

"That's how a lot of people find us. I'm Tessa, by the way."

I point to the name on the glass window. "The Tessa?"

"Yep, that's me."

"Cool."

I turn back and take the shot she pushes across the bar. "Thanks."

It's perfect, with a lovely layer of crema on top. I take a sip, enjoying the sweet acidity and the glorious bitterness, then I drink the rest quickly.

I have a man to find, so I leave Tessa to her adorable baking tasks or whatever and set across the street.

It's not as dark inside the bar as I expected. The exposed brick walls are painted white, and there are pot lights glowing in the ceiling as well as hanging fixtures with the Edison bulbs promised by the hipster name of the bar.

I love it immediately.

And then the man behind the bar moves, catching my attention, and everything else fades.

He's so tall it's hard to fully take him in. Well over six feet. Closer to seven, with big hands and bigger forearms and shoulders as wide as a football field. Beautiful brown skin covered in black ink.

"I'm looking for Bas." *Please be Bas.* The words shake as I say them, and wow, this is not going to go well. What was I thinking?

"You've found him."

"I..." My voice falters as my heart rate picks up. Nerves and excitement wrestle for top spot in my chest.

Then he holds out one of those hands—big, so big—and my heart just plain stops. "Sebastian Absalom, at your service."

I'm Meadow, I know I should say. I can hear it, a faint whisper.

An offer. Would it be too soon to fall to my knees and ask him to spank me?

Yes. Too soon.

One thing at a time. I hold out my hand and he shakes it gently, like he thinks I might break.

Okay, next task is to find my voice and convince him I'm not fragile. "Hi."

He smiles.

I nearly pass out.

Third task. Find more than a single syllable and introduce myself. *I'm Meadow. Financially independent, sexually curious, and very open to booty calls in the middle of the—*

Before I can say any of that, the bell above the door jangles again. Bas slides his gaze past me to the new arrival and his face lights up. Like, the smile he gave me before was nothing compared to this beaming welcome.

"Lovely," he says, moving around me. "I didn't know you were back in town."

Just like that, my spanking fantasies die a miserable, pathetic death.

And now I need to come up with an excellent excuse for why I showed up here looking for him.

"Sorry about that," he says from behind me. "Miss?"

I turn around, a falsely bright expression glued to my face. I can brass this out. No prob. "Yes?"

"Are you here for the apartment?"

My brain scrambles, latches on to the excuse, and instructs my head to nod agreeably. Yep. "I sure am. The apartment. Yes. That's me."

He tosses one of those big, inked arms around his girlfriend— ugh, I hate her already, which is totally unfair—and gives her a gentle squeeze. "Hang tight here while I show the place?"

She murmurs her agreement and slinks her way onto a

barstool. I viscerally and immediately dislike her, which is completely unreasonable. I'm sure she's lovely.

But she has a boyfriend with massive hands and I am about to find myself with two apartments when I barely use one.

Great.

Just, great.

"How did you find about the listing? It just went up?"

I can't tell him Max's name. Max said he talked to Bas about me. Fuck, can I even give him *my* name? What am I doing? "Uh… I think I saw someone share it online?"

"Cool."

Hardly. *Don't rent the apartment, Meadow.*

Except I will. I can feel it. I'm a thirty-year-old woman. A surgeon. And I'm about to do something completely stupid because of insta-lust over a brilliant smile and a pair of hands that make me weak in the knees.

Meadow Pedersen, you're a sucker.

2

BAS

Six months later

IT'S LATE when Meadow gets home. And by home, I mean the last barstool, the one closest to the stairs to her apartment.

She has an exterior entrance as well, but she only uses it when she's in a hurry.

When she hasn't had a completely shit day.

When she doesn't want to sit and have a drink in collegial silence.

Tonight is not that.

Tonight, I pour her a vodka tonic and set it in front of her. She drains it and wiggles her fingers, asking for another.

It takes all my willpower to not cover those wiggling fingers with my big paw, press her nervous little hands onto the bar, and make her say please.

But she's my customer. My tenant.

I don't get to demand manners from her.

It would be highly inappropriate to do so just to get a swift, sexual high from the exchange—one she would have no clue about.

So I stow my instincts deep and pour her another.

"That kind of day?" I finally ask, when she's nursing the bottom third of the glass and rolling her head back and forth.

"Yeah."

In the six months she's lived upstairs, we've gotten to know each other some. She probably knows me better than I know her, because I'm a talker and a dreamer, and Meadow is…not.

She's a listener.

She's probably a fucking amazing doctor. She listens and watches and doesn't miss a single thing.

She calls me on all my shit, and there's a lot of shit there to call out.

"Bas?"

"Yeah?"

"I said, how about your day?"

I swipe my towel across the new granite counter. "Ah. My day."

She narrows her eyes. Yeah, she sees everything. "What did you do?"

"Don't say it like that," I say, grinning at her. I'm charming. It's my saving grace.

But not with Meadow. She shakes her head. "What's the new project?"

"Project is an overstatement."

"Mmm-hmm." She swirls the last drop of her drink around the bottom of her glass. "Can I have one more?"

I love the earnest way she says it, like she'd accept it if I told her no. If I sent her packing off to bed for her own good, with a kiss on the tip of her upturned nose and a pat on her curvy bottom. "Yeah," I say instead, pouring her another drink.

"So, what was it?"

"It was nothing. Just an idea I had."

Her eyes dance as she watches me. Waiting. Knowing. "A good

distraction from the zoning change application you swore up and down you'd get done today?"

"Well, it's actually related to that."

"Mmm?" Her entire face lights up with the pure pleasure of knowing I'm full of shit, and I let her have that, because this has to be better than whatever happened at work that had her dragging when she came in.

"I was looking at the patio regulations, and I noticed a segment of the bylaws about licensing an entire street."

"An entire street," she repeats slowly.

I gesture out at the dark window to Duke Street. My little corner of Metcalfe, gloriously ungentrified. My corner of the capital region that I am entirely committed to improving, growing, making vibrant and amazing. "This street, for example."

"More than a patio?"

I nod. "A party. Maybe New Year's, although that competes with the city events. Or Halloween, although that would be kind of tight to pull together. But a street party would be a great way to give back to the community and connect with new business partners, and it would—could—make a good chunk of change if properly planned."

"A street party." She nods. "Interesting."

"Is it? Or are you humouring me?"

"Little of column A, little of column B? I don't know. I had a long day at the hospital and know next to nothing about business. But I think Halloween is a holiday relatively underserved in the adult population, if my university friends are anything to judge by. People love dressing up. Is that what you were thinking? Costumes, beer, that sort of thing?"

Yes, in the broadest of strokes. "Something like that. The details need to be sorted out, and I'll have to find—"

She bounces on her stool. "I'm in."

That catches me off-guard. "What?"

"I love Halloween, Bas." She leans across the bar, close enough

I can see the spray of freckles across her pale skin and count the individual eyelashes that brush against the apples of her cheeks. "Didn't you know that?"

"I did not."

She pushes back and grabs her glass. "Now you do." Tipping her head back, she drains the third drink. "Okay, that was probably two drinks too many, and I should hit the hay."

"Are you working tomorrow?" I don't know why I keep track. It doesn't matter. She'll come in when she wants a drink, text me when she needs something fixed.

As her landlord, I should not care if she's getting enough sleep.

She shakes her head. "Day off. Thankfully."

I'm relieved on her behalf, and I tap my palm against the counter. "All right. Sleep tight."

"Night," she says sweetly. "And I want to hear more about this street party tomorrow!"

"Come and find me," I say. "I'll probably be planning it most of the day, right here."

I watch as she hoists her backpack onto her shoulder and flips her dark red curls out of the way. That's all that's polite, so I pretend to go back to work as she moves away from the bar and heads to the door that separates the bar from the corridor that leads upstairs to the rental unit.

But I don't miss any of it. The way she takes a deep breath and pushes herself to the full extent of her small frame, like going to bed is a monumental task.

I've often wondered if it is. If the good doctor struggles with insomnia, but she's never said anything, and we don't have that kind of relationship.

We don't have any kind of relationship, really. I'm her landlord—and I need to remind myself of that fact every hour on the hour. But she's also slid into my life as a constant presence, even if it's all superficial. If I were any other kind of man, I would ask her out and see where it might go. And if she were any other kind of woman, maybe I might do it anyway, knowing that it likely wouldn't work out.

So I watch until she's through the door, then I turn my attention back to the bar. She was my last customer for the night. I clean up, then lock the front door and take the till back to the office to balance up the books. I'm eight bucks out, which I berate myself for.

I should hire staff. But that would require doing payroll, and I'm already overwhelmed by the quarterly tax forms and basic accounting for the audit I just know is coming someday.

I flash back five years, to the restlessness I often woke up with, that had driven me out of the city centre that day and landed me here, in this building, talking to a realtor who looked me up and down like he wasn't sure a guy like me could afford a building like this.

Except I could.

So I did—and I negotiated a hell of a deal in the end, too. Because that's the guy I am. Smart, adventurous, and way too impulsive for my own good, but just clever enough to yank my mistakes out of the fire at the last second and turn them into decent saves.

I still love the building, but I stopped loving the daily grind ages ago. I started looking for new projects a few years back. I've started too many to count, and let nearly all of them fall by the wayside.

I'm untethered. Unfocused.

There is a strong argument to be made that I should focus on the bar, which has always been my strength. Listening, talking, selling.

My computer screen goes dark, sliding into a set of generic screensaver images. I click on the mouse and scowl at the screen. Accounting is not my forte. And when the bookkeeping program closes, behind it is the still incomplete zoning application.

No, Meadow, I didn't do what I set out to accomplish today. I fucked around with a harebrained idea and pushed today's to-do list to tomorrow.

I promise myself that I'll finish the application in the morning.

Before I plan a street party.

Before I get distracted by my tenant's teasing, knowing looks that make me want to cover her mouth and really give her something to be surprised by.

3

MEADOW

IT'S bright outside when I finally wake up. Oh, I how I love a day off after a couple of shifts in a row. Rolling over, I grab my phone and do a quick check of my messages while I stumble to the bathroom.

After a long, hot shower, I twist my hair up into a bun, then throw on some comfy clothes. Coffee is in my immediate future. A giant, frothy latte made by Tessa at the shop across the street— the third best thing about this apartment.

The first is just how big it is, and since I don't have much stuff here, I get to enjoy the spacious expanse of it.

The second is that Bas is always downstairs with a ready smile for me.

With that in mind, I order him a coffee, too. While I'm waiting for those, I let Tessa draw me into a conversation. She's just stuck her daily Tarot card on the wall. She likes to do a card reading for herself every morning after the rush.

"Why don't you do it first thing?" I ask her.

"Some days, that early in the morning still feels like the day before, if that makes sense? And it's so hectic and rushed. My mind isn't clear and focused. And it's something fun to do at my first lull." She grins. "You want me to do a reading for you?"

I shake my head. "I'm good."

"All right. Here you go, two lattes. You got your muffins already?"

I raise the paper bag. "Yep."

"Have a great day, Meadow."

"You too!"

Conversations like that make up for the thirty-minute commute into the city.

As does the view when I go to find Bas in his office. Technically, he lives in the other apartment upstairs, but this is his domain—a large, light-filled space behind the bar, with a gorgeous desk and a big-ass leather executive chair behind it, large enough for all of him and his smile, too.

He rocks back on the chair and spreads his arms wide. "How did you know I haven't had coffee yet today?"

"A lucky guess," I murmur as I hand his latte over to him. Even after six months, there's still a sizzle against my skin when his fingers brush mine. I ignore it. We're well past that.

A lovely friendship is way better than an unrequited crush.

"Are you working on the street party idea?" I curl up in the chair across from his desk and nod at the scatter of papers between us, all covered in pencil sketches of Duke Street, with the various shops on either side. "And also, how have you been this productive without caffeine?"

"I run on enthusiasm," he says, like that's normal.

My enthusiasm was murdered somewhere in the third year of residency. "I'm jealous," I admit.

His brows pull together as he looks at me. "You okay?"

I smile brightly. It doesn't matter. I still love my job. It's just not party-planning level of fun. "Yep. So, Halloween is a go?"

"I think so." He shrugs. "I'm just playing around with it. Not a big deal. Maybe it would be better to throw it at someone else. I'll see if Tessa wants to do it."

I swallow back the criticism that jumps to the tip of my tongue. It's not my place to say, *no, don't give this up!*

There's so much to adore about Bas. His fire, his protectiveness, and the way he looks at you and everything else in the world disappears. Poof. It's just you and him, and it would be so easy to get caught up in that.

Hell, I did, in a single second, when I first met him.

But.

But.

The man can't commit to a single woman, a single plan, a single anything to save his life. He's constantly coming up with the next great idea, and then he drops it—or hands it off to someone else—as soon as he gets bored.

I can't imagine how much it would hurt to be handed off because he got bored of me.

No. That's a lie. I can imagine, and that's why I've never acted on my feelings for him.

My phone vibrates. I glance at the screen. It's my cleaning lady.

"Sorry," I say to Bas, sliding off the stool. "I have to get this."

"Work comes first." He grins.

I don't correct him. Outside, I take a deep breath and answer the phone. "This is Meadow."

"Sorry to bother you, Ms. Pedersen. I've just finished cleaning the unit and the previous guests seem to have taken the hairdryer with them."

I sigh. "Okay, thanks for letting me know."

"Would you like me to pick up a replacement?"

I shake my head even though she can't see me. "It's all right. I've got the day off, and it's been a while since I've visited the condo. I'll do it."

Ending the call, I make sure my phone is on silent and head back inside.

"Everything okay?" Bas asks.

"Yep." I slide back into my chair. "I need to head downtown in a bit. Something came up but it won't take me long. I've got some time to finish going over the plans with you, if you want help."

His warm gaze slides over my face. That right there. It's scary how good it feels having his full attention. "You really like this idea, eh?"

"Yep."

"Good."

"If you want to give it to Tessa, I bet she'd be all over it."

He strokes his beard slowly. My eyes catch on the hypnotic slide of his thick fingers against his skin. "No," he says. "I think I want to keep this for myself. If you're going to help me, that is."

My breath catches in my throat and I nod. "Count me in."

4

BAS

By the end of the week, I've spoken to all the business owners on the street. Tessa at the coffee shop and Mabel from Weirdaker Games at the other end of Duke Street have both agreed to write a letter of support for my street party zoning application.

When I'm across the street at Tessa's getting her signature, she runs over her plans for a stall.

"It may be basic," she warns me. "I don't want to do a ton of baking for the end of the day if we don't have a clear idea for turnout numbers."

"Basic is fine." It's what I usually serve at the bar. Pretzels, bowls of nuts, cheese plates.

"We could do candy. Trick or treat at each stall. It technically contributes to the requirements of having food on hand to go with the alcohol."

I laugh out loud, grab my phone, and text Meadow to get her thoughts.

Bas: What do you think about trick-or-treating at all the stalls?

Meadow: Yes! Sugar highs are not a problem for grown-up trick-or-treaters.

I repeat that line to Tessa, and she agrees. While I was texting, she picked up her Tarot deck. She notices that I noticed, and holds it out. "Do you want a reading?"

I shake my head. "Nah. Another time, I've still got a lot of planning to do and a bar to run."

Something about Meadow's text continues to whirl around in my mind as I walk back to the bar.

Grown-up trick or treaters.

Grown-up.

I rub my hand over my jaw.

One way to get a good minimum number of people to turn out, people who would buy food from the coffee shop and keep me in good standing with a business neighbour, would be to invite a bunch of community groups with large volunteer pools. I happen to know a few of those circles.

Free tables for any non-profit group. I rap my knuckles on my desk and open a new email window.

THE RESPONSE IS OVERWHELMING. And through the grapevine come requests for paying tables, too, from vendors in the city who are tired of fighting for overpriced event opportunities there.

I set up an application form on Saturday. By Sunday, I have thirty interested vendors and there's only enough space for twenty in the requested licensed area.

"That's a good problem to have," Meadow says as she slowly

picks at a muffin in the doorway to my office Monday afternoon. "Isn't it?"

I tug on my short-cropped beard. Not short-cropped enough right now. I've been distracted by the street party planning and haven't trimmed it in a few weeks. "I don't want to burn any bridges. But on the other hand, I want the event to seem like an in-demand booking. Right now, I've confirmed ten vendors and put the rest on a waiting list. I'll pull most off the list in the end, I think. We can have a second row of vendors outside the licensed area, around the corner."

She nods slowly. "Cool. What else do you have planned?"

I flip through my notes. "Outdoor heaters, because some of the costumes will be…risqué, I bet."

"Like, how risqué are we talking?" Her foot thunks against the door frame as she stands more at attention. "Because right now, my costume plan is pretty pedestrian, and if I need to step up my game, I need time to get organized."

"It's not a contest." Definitely not a contest. One of the vendors asked that, because they wanted to sponsor a prize. Nuh. Not my style to judge people as better or hotter than others. I want this to be as inclusive as possible. "Be your adorable self and don't worry about how dirty other costumes get."

"I'm not worried," she says frostily. "But good to know you think I'm adorable."

The way she says it pricks at me, and I lift my head to look at her.

Oh yeah, that's a familiar glare. No woman wants to be told she's not sexy. I give her a grin. "Sorry. You're sexy as hell, Meadow. It's all good. Wear whatever you want."

Her nose is still out of joint, though. She drops her hands, her muffin forgotten now. "I feel like this party has changed significantly from the funtimes beer garden of last week."

"I guess it has." I shrug. I don't care if things are sliding around. That's life. Great ideas emerge from chaos. "Maybe hold off until we finalize the theme and announce the list of vendors. But because you're my friend, I'll give you a heads up—there will be some fetish wear in the mix. Lots of role-play type costumes."

"Kinky stuff?" She doesn't blink.

Meadow—the good doctor, the sweet tenant—doesn't blink at kinky costumes.

I guess one sees everything at the hospital, but I was expecting her to squirm a little.

Deep down, I'm a little disappointed she didn't, which is fucked up. It's good that she's cool with whatever. "Yep."

"Huh." She looks at me, eyes narrowed. "That is a change."

"Kind of developed over the weekend while you were working."

"Interesting." Then she smiles, her eyes twinkling, and leans in. "Can you imagine me as a Domme, Bas?"

My mouth runs dry. No, I can't. Not even a little bit. I can see her in a collar, naked except for a small strip of leather stamped Property of Absalom. I can see her in a 1950's pin-up girl costume, walking funny because I make her put a plug in her sweet, round ass before she goes out to play.

I can see her in any number of submissive costumes.

None of them are appropriate for me to suggest, so it's good that she giggles and shakes her head. "Oh, man, the look on your face." She goes back to nibbling on her muffin, frostiness gone, and I choose discretion over trying to explain anything.

I don't have a good explanation.

I do, however, have a semi-hard dick. And it's interfering with my ability to think clearly, so when she finishes her snack, and says she's heading upstairs to nap, I forget to tell her that I know a lot of the people who will come to the party.

I've played with a fair number of them. In dungeons and at sex parties.

Hey, so, your landlord is a dirty dog, and you might want to re-

think joking about sexy costumes with him. Also, he'd totally under-stand if you're re-thinking the entire friendship.

Except that would be a lie. I'd fucking hate that.

I should tell her sooner than later. Ease her into the idea that I have a darker side, but it's no big deal.

And my fantasies—of the collar, of a rosy pink ass, or a cute little bunny tail wiggling at me as she hops away—will stay safely locked up.

What Meadow wears to the street party is entirely up to Meadow—and none of my business.

5

MEADOW

THE ABSOLUTE BEST part of my job is delivering babies, and tonight we have a full house on the delivery ward. There are three women in active labour, two inductions in the early stages, and at least one woman on antenatal that we're watching and might take in for a c-section later if her bloodwork changes.

There's a fine balance in medicine between watching the numbers, trusting the numbers, and making the gut call to ignore the numbers because your Spidey Sense says this one isn't like the others. That sense gets stronger over time. I've seen some consultants with decades of experience make some whacked out calls—and be right—because their internal reference database is just that varied.

I'm relatively new to this. My internal reference database is a picture-perfect memory of all the recent evidence published in peer-reviewed journals.

I'm a barrel of fun at parties.

Speaking of which…I still don't have a costume for Bas's street party. His *kinky* street party, although he hasn't been more forthcoming about that aspect of it. But I got the gist. I also picked up, loud and clear, that he doesn't think that's my scene.

I'm going to prove him wrong. I'll show him I'm a hell of a lot more than *adorable.* There was something about that exchange that pushed me off the awkward should-I, shouldn't-I fence I've been teetering on for the last couple of months.

I should.

I should tell him how I feel.

I should admit the deception I fell into when we met.

I should tell him the truth, because in the end, if I don't, our friendship isn't real.

A tremor of fear ripples through me at the thought of losing what we have—but what we currently have isn't what I really want. And he's friends with a lot of his exes. Why couldn't he be friends with the girl who had a crush on him, lied to him, and moved into his apartment like a perverted stalker? If I don't frame it that way, of course, because yikes.

I'll need to work on my presentation of the truth.

One thing at a time. First, a sexy costume and a way to make it clear to him that I'm not the little miss goody-two-shoes he's pegged me as. Second, I'll make it clear I want him. Third, I'll admit that's been the truth from the moment we met.

"It's a good plan," I say out loud, under my breath.

"The induction in room 3?" the resident next to me asks.

I glance up the white board, and the progress stats. Yep, that's a good plan, too. "Mm-hmm. I'm going to take a few minutes and do some Halloween shopping, all right? Page me if anything changes."

"Sure thing."

The staff lounge is empty, so I stay there instead of heading all the way to my office. I fire up my laptop and Google *sexy adult Halloween costumes*. Then I immediately close that window, because no, not that sexy—this is still a public street event, after all—and I try again.

Classy kinky costumes doesn't return better results.

But then, on the side, I see an ad for a store selling corsets, and when I click on that, a whole array of options present themselves. Cosplay. Steampunk. And then I see a tutu.

It's been fifteen years since I last wore a ballet leotard, but for the decade before that it was practically a second skin to me.

That's something sexy and possibly kinky that I would feel comfortable wearing in public. And on the same page is a link to ballet-styled boots, which make a lot more sense for an Ontario Halloween—and an outdoor street festival any time of the year—than slippers would. Done, and done.

I quickly add the tutu, the boots, some fishnet stockings, and two kinds of body leotards to my cart, because a girl likes options when it comes to baring skin. Then I pick a corset which, if I weren't wearing a leotard, would bare more than just the tops of my breasts.

It's a filthy costume that makes me feel funny.

It's perfect.

As I push the order button, the lounge door swings open and a woman I don't know walks in. She's in scrubs and her badge says Dr. Addison Greer, Paediatrics. I catch all of that in the split second before I close my laptop, a little too quickly to be casual.

She skids to a halt. "Sorry, am I interrupting something?"

I laugh nervously. "Nope."

"I can come back."

"It's fine." I hold my breath for a second. "Actually, I just want to make sure an order went through. It's a Halloween costume, nothing inappropriate." Not too inappropriate, anyway. Not in its individual parts.

"Averting my eyes," she says gently, swivelling away from me. "I'm Addison, by the way. I'm new to the Paeds team. I'm covering Max Donovan's shift tonight. And I adore Halloween costumes, so the dorkier the better."

"This is less dorky and more trying-to-impress-a-man," I admit. "Which is a weird thing to share with a new colleague, but I'm sure Max will tell you have a tendency to put my foot in my mouth about all sorts of things." I open my computer, double-check the order went through, then stow it away in my messenger bag.

I stand up. "You can turn around again." I hold out my hand. "Meadow Pedersen. Obstetrics."

She beams and squeezes my fingers gently. "Max said I'd like working with you, and he wasn't wrong."

"Have you had a look at the board? We're going to have a busy night." As I say that, my pager goes off. I sling my messenger bag across my body and point in the general direction of the nursing station. "Shall we?"

"After you."

"Where did you come from before here?"

"Colorado. Before that, I was in B.C. That's where I know Max from."

"Neat." And with that, we're into the thick of it. One mom has started pushing, another is in a nice holding pattern, having a wee rest before she gets started. I stash my bag under the desk, re-tuck my curls into a tight bun on the back of my head, and take a deep breath.

It's time to welcome some new people into the world.

6

BAS

A WEEK BEFORE HALLOWEEN, a courier driver comes into the bar late afternoon. "I've got a package for a Meadow Pedersen," he says, totally ignoring the fact he's in a bar and I don't look like my name is Meadow.

It's possible, of course. So I play it that way. "That's me," I say dryly.

The dude doesn't even blink. "Sign here."

I want to give him a fist bump for being cool about identity, but just in case he's simply bored out of his gourd, I don't bother. Instead I scrawl something that could be Meadow, but could also be Absalom, and take the box from him.

It's surprisingly heavy.

I text the intended recipient.

Bas: Got a delivery to the bar for you.
Meadow: I'm on call until tomorrow morning, and sticking close to the hospital. Can you put it upstairs for me?
Bas: Sure thing.
Meadow: Thanks.

She adds a flower emoji.

Fucking cute as hell. I send back a grinning devil, because flowers aren't my speed, and truck upstairs.

Even after six months of living in my rental unit, Meadow doesn't have much stuff. She's barely here, to be fair. She seems to live at the hospital, often sleeping there. Today being a good case in point.

But the poor woman doesn't have much furniture, either. The front room is massive, and has enough space for a full living room set, but she only has one small love seat. Of course, she's just one small person, living here all by herself, and she never has anyone over.

But still.

I wonder about that every time I'm in here, which isn't that often. Mail deliveries like this, the occasional landlord repair issue.

Her couches, or lack thereof, are not my problem. I leave the package just inside her front door, lock up carefully, and head downstairs to tend bar and daydream about the street party.

When I get back downstairs, the bar phone is ringing.

I grab the handset loosely and put it to my ear. "Duke and Main, how can I help you?"

"Bas," a woman's voice snaps crisply in my ear.

I smile, recognizing my favourite cop from the first syllable. "Corrine, what can I do for you?"

"Your little street party has grabbed some high-level attention."

"In a good way or a bad way?"

"In a *the prime minister talked about attending* kind of way."

As much as *I* would get a kick out of the nation's leader drinking my beer next to a guy dressed head-to-toe in latex, I can't imagine that would be a good look on the next days' morning news. "That's not a good idea."

"We realize that," she says dryly. "And he realizes it too, but it came up at a meeting, and some of the people in attendance are talking about coming, and while we can run interference on the PM's calendar, everyone else in this town is a private citizen. So I need a favour from you."

"Anything."

"Can I come out there and get a walk through on the plan? Unofficially. Low-key."

Cabinet ministers, I'm assuming. From what little I know about Corinne's job, it sounds awful. A lifelong capital region RCMP officer, she recently transferred onto the Prime Minister's security detail and now she's a glorified babysitter.

This conversation is a prime example. "My plan is your plan, my lovely."

She chuckles. "I'm not your lovely anymore."

No. That hadn't worked out between us. "Are you still seeing those two guys from the Senators?"

"Nope. I'm enjoying some me time right now. I'll tell you all about it when I see you."

SHE COMES around the next night, around nine. The bar is busy enough, but I'm between customers when the door opens and Corinne stalks in. She's wearing snug jeans and a leather jacket, with heavy boots on her feet, and carrying a helmet.

"Cold night for a ride," I say as she tugs off her gloves and sets them on the bar.

"Nice and brisk," she says with a grin. "How's it going?"

I shrug. "It's going."

She searches my face, then nods. I don't give her anything else. We're not close friends. Mostly acquaintances through the kink community, who dated for a short while and figured out we weren't compatible that way. And now she's here in a professional capacity, so I'm not going to do a deep dive into all the ways I'm dissatisfied with my life.

None of her business. "Do you want a drink?"

"I'd take a Coke."

"For sure." I pour her a tall glass and add a lime to the rim. "So, what do you need to know?"

"Do you have a map of the street party perimeter?"

I pull a sketch out from under the bar and slide it across to her. "I'm having this printed up as well, but here's the rough draft."

"Flying by the seat of your pants, eh?" Another grin, and I frown. Nothing wrong with her observation, and it's true, but it grates at me. Yeah, I do a lot of shit last minute. But I get it done, and it's my fucking party. She taps her fingers on the zigzag marks I've used to denote where the perimeter fencing will be. "This will essentially seal in the space, except for the official entrances?"

I nod. "Basically."

"It's the not-so-basically parts I'm curious about. The secret back exits out of places like this bar." She looks to the rear of my building, and everything connects in my head.

She wants to know where she can smuggle a VIP out if shit-disturbing bloggers show up or something. Okay. I grab a red marker and draw all the possible exit lines on top of my sketch. "Official entrances are here and here, at either end. Those will be staffed for the entire duration of the event. These four businesses —" I point to my bar, the coffee shop, the gaming company at the other end of the street that is doing an escape room haunted house, and the gift shop across the street from that. "We are all open all night, mostly for people to use the facilities because we decided porta-potties are disgusting."

Corinne laughs. "Good call."

"Each building has a back entrance. So those are all options. On this side of the street—my bar, and the gift shop—there's an alley that runs the full length. That's a bit better for car access, if you need it. But the other side, you can walk to a side street pretty quickly."

She scrubs a hand over her face and sighs, I'm assuming in relief. "Great."

"Tell me to mind my own business if you want, but who's your big concern? If I can help out and keep my eyes open, I'm happy to. I want this to go off without a hitch."

A long, pregnant pause stretches before she nods. "All right. Ellie Strong wants to come to your street party."

I choke on a laugh. "The prime minister's *wife?*"

Corinne's mouth twitches. "She's been stir-crazy at home with the baby, and thought it would be fun."

"So when you said it came up in a meeting…"

"I mean a dinner party at 24 Sussex."

"Ah." I scratch my beard. "You don't want to just tell her that she can't come?"

"The only person who might get away with that is the PM, and he has given his blessing for her to do whatever she wants in this regard. He agreed not to come himself—that adds too much —but if she wants to have a girls' night out with her friends, that's her right."

Everyone else in this town is a private citizen. It's a stretch, but I support the principle of the idea. "All right. What do I need to know?"

Her face gets serious. "Look, Ellie doesn't want to bring any drama to your event, or any embarrassment to her husband's office. But she has a right to live her life freely and fully, and it's my job to make sure she can do that without making too big of a fuss about it. Understood?"

Completely. I begin rearranging the street plan in my head. I'm going to need some help here. An outside perspective. A woman's input. "I'm on it."

Corinne reaches across the bar and wraps her hand over my

forearm. "You are a gem." Her lips twitch, but she doesn't let me in on the private joke. "Don't clean it up entirely, all right? Let the woman have some fun."

"I'll walk the line and keep it on the entertaining side of depraved."

"Perfect." Her fingers slide against my arm and I catch her hand in mine and give it a small squeeze before she leans back and grabs her gloves. But she doesn't leave right away. "So the rumours are true? The whole kink community is turning out?"

"That's what I hear. Is that going to be okay with Ellie Strong."

She tips her head back and laughs. "Yeah," she finally says. "It'll be okay."

"What will be okay?" We both turn as one.

I should have seen Meadow arrive. I don't know why I didn't.

Corinne sizes her up, and I made the safest introduction I can imagine. "Meadow, this is Corinne, an old friend who will be coming to the street party. Corinne, this is Meadow. We met when she rented the room upstairs, and she's been a great support with planning the party."

As far as intros go, it's not bad.

But it's not as safe as I expect, either. Meadow frowns. "I haven't helped that much."

"Moral support," I reassure her. "Speaking of which, how was your day? Want a drink?"

She glances at Corinne. "No, I'm going to head to bed. Nice to meet you."

The cop barely has a chance to respond in kind before my tenant is gone in a tiny ball of blazing curls and obvious huff.

"I, uh…" I shrug. "She's a doctor. Sometimes her shifts are brutal. She's lovely, though."

Corinne gives me an appraising look. "I have no doubt."

I swallow a defence of Meadow. For one thing, she doesn't need it. And for another, she's none of Corinne's business. Instead I turn back to what *is* her business—the tightrope walk we're about to embark on. "I'm going to do some work on this tonight. Look for an email from me with the relevant details tomorrow. And if you have any sway over Mrs. Strong's costume—"

"None."

"In that case, I'll keep my thoughts to myself."

"For the best." She pulls her gloves back on and grabs her helmet. "For what it's worth, your Meadow wasn't tired just there. She was jealous. And we both know there was no reason for it, so you could share your thoughts on *that* with *her*, if you were in the mood to talk about something."

I laugh, because she's wrong.

Corinne shrugs. "I'm telling you, a woman knows when she's being sized up as competition."

"You're not competition," I insist, and damn if that doesn't reveal more than I meant. "Go away. Please. I need to look after some things."

She smiles and takes her leave.

I raise my voice and tell the guys at the back of the bar that it's last call.

"What the hell, man? It's not even ten!" one of them hollers back.

"Personal emergency."

They grumble, but they also bring their glasses to the bar on their way out. Good guys. "Next round is on me," I promise, and they wave before following Corinne out the front door.

I stalk in the same direction and lock up behind them.

Duke and Main is closed for the night.

After turning off the lights, I take a deep breath, try to unscramble my thoughts—unsuccessfully—and take the stairs up to Meadow's apartment two at a time.

She answers on the second knock. She's changed into leggings and a t-shirt that's too big for her. Her face is bare and her hair is piled up in a bun on top of her head.

Something clenches hard inside my chest. Something that feels a hell of a lot like stupidity.

She doesn't say anything, so it's on me to lead this.

Fuck. I clear my throat and start with safe. "You got your package."

She's polite in return. "I did. Right where you left it."

"Good."

"Good." Then she sighs, because she's braver than I am. "It's late, Bas."

"It's not. I'll tell you how I know it's not late. I just had to kick two guys out who wanted to stay and drink for a few more hours, but honestly, I don't give a fuck about that."

"You closed the bar?"

"I wanted to talk to you." I wait a beat, searching her face. "Unless it really is late, and you have to get up in four hours, and then I'll go and open up again."

She swings the door wide open. "Come on in."

7

MEADOW

IT'S BEEN a while since Bas has been up here. He showed me the place when I rented it, gave me the keys when I moved in, and he came up twice to fix things in sexy landlord style.

He's never come up to talk.

I always go to him. Follow him around like a lovesick puppy—which he ignores like a boss. So, I don't know, I guess I got complacent.

Obviously, my little flounce out of the bar was noticed. I probably offended his new friend.

The one he was touching.

Gah, I'm a sucker. A sucker who has been paying for two homes for six months, although the AirBnB guests enjoying my condo downtown more than cover the mortgage.

But still. I moved out to the sticks for a pair of big hands and a gorgeous smile, and tonight I saw those hands on someone else—totally his right, because *I'm nothing to him*—and now he's going to lecture me about boundaries or something.

Let's get it over with.

And maybe I'll move out, because who needs a thirty-minute commute anyway?

"What's up?" I ask as he follows me into my empty living room.

I may be the sucker who'll pay for two homes. I won't buy extra furniture. Now I've got two apartments with half the usual amount of stuff in each.

Good thing I like a spartan aesthetic.

"I think we've got something we need to discuss. Between us."

"Sure," I say breezily. I'm not looking at him. Something I've learned through medical school and residency is take feedback with a certain detachment. It's just data. Just information. Not personal.

Even when it's painfully personal.

"Do you want coffee? Tea?" I lead him into the kitchen and reach for the kettle. I don't even have a coffee maker here, but I can do a pour over if I need to. Hell, it's still early enough that the coffee shop across the street might be open. "We could go over to—"

"I want to clear the air." His voice is low and rough, like he's not fucking around.

I turn to look at him, almost against my will. But I can't *not* look at him a second longer.

He fills the doorway.

Great, I've trapped myself in the kitchen with someone three times my size, not that Bas is scary. No, he's not frightening. But the look on his face is terrifying in a different way.

In a real, emotional way.

Like he knows he's going to break my heart. So maybe he has been paying attention all this time.

God. I don't want to do this. I don't want to hear whatever it is, except I invited him in. "About what?" I manage to squeak.

"What you saw downstairs, to start." He frowns, his brows pulling hard over his dark, piercing eyes. "That was work."

"Great. Good."

"That was *just* work," he repeats, stepping towards me.

I back up, bumping into the counter. "You don't need to explain that to me."

His gaze drills deep against me. "Except I think I do, for some reason."

"Oh." This is the part where he lets me down easy. Or not so easy. His look isn't very sympathetic right now. "Are you mad at me?"

"Pardon?" His face gets even tighter. "No, I'm not mad at you, Meadow."

My hand shakes as I lift my arm and point my index finger at his eyebrows. "That's not a happy look."

He blinks. And frowns even further. I don't think it's possible for a human being to look angrier than he looks right now.

But he's still not scary.

He flicks his gaze from my face to my finger—still pointing at him—and then back to my face. "There's a mile of other feelings between happy and angry," he finally grates out.

"Oh."

"I feel like I missed something, at some point, and it's important. So I'm going to say this again. What you saw downstairs was work."

"She was touching you," I blurt out.

"She's an ex."

"They're all exes."

His eyes go wide, and well, there it is, I guess. In for a penny…

I swallow hard. "You have an endless parade of exes. And they all touch you."

"You've noticed?"

"I spend a lot of time in your bar, Bas. Yes, I notice. It's right in front of me."

"You've never said anything."

I take a deep breath. "No, I haven't."

"Do you want to say something now?"

My heart hammers against my ribs. Not really. "You seem to

have a type. I mean, if one were a casual observer of all things Bas, one might notice some consistency on that front."

"And you might be that kind of casual observer?"

I nod.

He moves closer, and my hand—still between us—pushes against his chest. Or his chest presses into my fingers, curling them into a soft fist between us. He leans in and rests his hands on the counter on either side of me.

I'm still not scared of him. Scared of my feelings, absolutely. Scared of being rejected, even, which is starting to feel a bit silly.

If he was going to reject me his mouth wouldn't be this close.

His perfect, soft, full lips.

His white teeth, set in a straight line as he smiles at me.

"You don't look mad anymore," I whisper.

"I'm not angry. I told you that." His voice is soft and quiet now, too. Like we're exchanging secrets. "I had no idea you were watching me."

"I didn't want you to know."

"Why not?" His hot gaze pins me down. Like I can't escape his inspection.

"There was always someone else. And when there wasn't, you were…uninterested."

Something dark flickers in his eyes, and a corresponding hard tug deep inside me responds.

I remember back to how I landed here in the first place. Max had told Bas about me, and then suggested I look him up. Bas was looking for someone just like me, but I chickened out. Maybe it wasn't too late to follow up on that. "Did I give you the impression that I might not be the girl for you, Bas? Because I like you. A lot. I want you. A lot."

He laughs, a harsh, unexpected sound that ricochets around my kitchen. It sends a shiver down my spine and makes my thighs quiver. "That could be a dangerous proposition."

"Maybe I like danger."

"Whoa," he whispers, his face softening. "Hang on, that wasn't what I meant. I'm not any kind of threat to you, sweetness. Okay?"

Now it's my turn to laugh, a nervous giggle. "I wasn't opposed to the dangerous proposition."

He sways over me, his mouth twisting in a matching smile. "I heard that."

My heart rate is now speeding along like a freight train. "Am I doing this all wrong?"

He shakes his head. "Nope."

"I mean, we haven't even kissed yet, and I'm telling you I want you to…"

His eyes search my face as I trail off. "Yes?"

My cheeks turn pink. "I don't know."

"Should we start with a kiss, then?"

The freight train in my chest slams into a mountain of need. "Yes, please."

Using his index finger, he tips my chin up and gently brushes his lips to mine. I've waited so long for this. I open to him, eagerly. He tastes me first, a hungry slide of tongue against tongue. It's rough and soft at the same time, commanding and delicious. When his licks slow, I suckle on his tongue gently, playing with it. He groans and squeezes my waist, then drops his hand to my hip.

So close to my ass. But he doesn't palm it, doesn't squeeze it.

No spanks for me, because neither of us are psychic.

And there's at least a part of Bas that is sweet, because he rubs my hip and lifts his hand back to my chin, easing out of our lingering, amazing kiss. "That's probably enough for tonight."

"What? No." I tug on his shoulders and brush my lips against his jaw. "Get back here. I want more."

"Or we can take it easy and—"

"I've wanted to use you as a sex toy for six months. We don't need to wait a second longer."

He groans and shakes his head. "Please stop talking. If I'm going to leave, you've gotta—"

"I imagined your fingers inside me for ages. Why would I want you to leave?" I glare up at him, feeling bright and bold and challenging. Fearless. "I imagined your tongue on me—"

"That's enough," He growls, hooking his fingers into the front of my jeans. My skin sizzles under his touch.

With his thumb, he flicks the button free. Then he wrenches the zipper down and peels the denim open. He whispers my name as he strokes the bare skin of my belly, and he crushes his mouth against mine again. This kiss is hard and fast, obscene and demanding.

As his lips work against mine, he teases with is tongue, licking and thrusting. I'm taking this as a promise of what it will feel like between my legs. And his fingers get as far as my panties before he stops again.

This time, he doesn't pull away.

He just stops.

I can feel how conflicted he is. And I know it's a big, hard conflict, because there's something big and hard pressing against my hip. I rub against his erection and he groans again.

"Here's the thing," he says, his breath ragged and his eyes wild as he looks down at me. "I want to take you to bed now. I want to stay there for a week and talk about all the filthy things you want me to do to you. But we don't have that kind of time right now, and I have to re-design a street party to accommodate the wife of the prime minister getting her public kink on in a safe-for-public consumption way."

"What?"

"That's what Corinne was here about." He kisses me again. "I want your help with that, if you're willing?"

I'm the textbook definition of willing, for anything and every-thing Bas might want. "Sure." I still don't quite follow. One minute we were making out and his fingers were an inch away from my clit. Now he's talking about the street party. "Why can't we have sex?"

"Because you've watched me, Meadow. You know I'm a shitty boyfriend. I ghost women when I do a deep dive into projects. I forget dates. And nobody minds that much, because everyone has my number, and it's no big deal when we drift in different directions. You've seen all of that, right?"

I blink at him. Yeah, I have. And yes, that's how I'd sum it all up.

But wouldn't we be different?

He cups my face in his hands. His big, warm, sexy hands, which I've wanted on my body for months now. And he sighs. "I don't want to be that guy for you. I'm not that guy, not always. I'll tell you all about that some other time. But tonight, I want you to go to sleep knowing I won't hurt you. That I'll wait until I can give you my all."

"So sex will be next week?"

He grins. "Halloween, if you want."

I have to work tomorrow. And I don't have to work the day after the street party. This is a good plan.

My body doesn't agree. My body wants Bas now, in whatever way we can get him.

But he's right. We should take things a bit slower. Spend a week kissing and talking, and then there's the small matter of me coming clean about how I wound up in his apartment... "Okay," I whisper as he brushes his lips against mine again. "Next week. And yes, I'll help you clean up your dirty street party."

"An hour ago I thought you were the right person to consult on all things sweet," he murmurs. "And then you said those filthy things about what you want me to do to you..."

I roll my eyes. "If you don't think the PM and his wife are super dirty, I've got some news for you."

He shakes his head. "Don't tell me."

"The way they look at each other..."

Bas presses his forehead against mine. "You're telling me anyway."

I smile. "And I know some people who know him." *Max, who knows Bas too, but now is not the time to admit that.* "And they strike me as kinky, too. I don't know. I just get the feeling."

He shrugs his big, broad shoulders. "And I know people who are for sure kinky around the PM, and they've never said anything, so who knows. But it's as good a theory as any, so let's go on that idea: Mrs. Strong is secretly kinky, and can't explore that in public most of the time. So how do we make the whole thing safe for public news consumption but also delightfully perverted for everyone, including a VIP?"

8

BAS

My principles carry me as far as my own apartment. As soon as I close the door behind me, I lift my hand to my face and breathe in the scent of Meadow on my fingers.

Fuck. I deserve a medal for not fucking her tonight.

But she has to work in the morning—which means leaving at five. I'm not selfishly robbing her sleep because I want to get inside her body.

We're going to take some time. Do this right. Talk more, kiss more, and when we have all the time in the world, we'll take it to the next level.

"I've wanted to use you as a sex toy for six months."

My cock throbs as Meadow's words ring in my ears. There's so much about this woman I still need to discover so we can do this right. *This.* I don't even know what it is, but I know it's different. I want a relationship with Meadow—what we already have, plus kinky sex. I want to tie her up, hold her down, make her scream.

I usually date inside the kink-familiar pool of Ottawa submissives. Kink first, chemistry second. And honestly, until Meadow bounced into my bar, I didn't care that much about chemistry. A good scene could work with anyone. Negotiate, do the thing, mutually get off, and be done with it. Rinse and repeat until it got boring.

Maybe I missed an opportunity tonight to explain that to Meadow. *All those women were basically friends with benefits. Bondage benefits, discipline benefits...*

But does she need to know that level of detail about my past when maybe it doesn't matter for her? Because with Meadow, it's all chemistry. I'm not thinking about scenes. I'm thinking about skin and moans, sleepy fucking and naked cuddling.

I lean back against the door and palm my cock through my jeans. Cuddling that might lead to wrestling. Pinning her down and forcing her legs open. Sweet, pale thighs. Dark red curls and pink, wet skin.

A hand on her arm, another on her leg. Dragging my cock through her slick folds. Whispering all sorts of filthy threats.

Her eyes, bright. Challenging. Her mouth just as dirty as mine.

That was the best surprise of tonight. Meadow isn't meek in the least. She wants things.

I shudder as I squeeze the aching crown of my dick.

Fuck.

Flipping off the lights, I unzip my jeans and throw myself onto my couch. It doesn't take long. A few rough jerks, then a faster stroke. Meadow's words rocketing around in my brain.

My dirty, sweet, good little one.

I'm going to make the next week so good for her. Waiting will be delicious.

BUT MEADOW DOESN'T COME HOME the next night. She's on a twenty-four hour shift at the hospital and sticking close there, she says in a text.

Then she sends me a follow-up cartoon image of a woman wiggling out of her panties.

Bas: That's delightfully filthy.
Meadow: It's my secret after-dark brand.
Bas: I like it just as much as your public brand.
Meadow: I gotta go. ORs don't wait for sexting.

Surgery also interferes with me telling her about *my* secret after-dark brand. And when she comes home the next day it's to sleep. By the time she wakes up, I'm behind the bar.

That doesn't stop me from kissing her. I drag her behind the bar and hold her close, savouring the feel of her body in my arms, her lips against mine. And when she cheerily perches on a stool across from me, I make a silent pledge to hire a part-time bartender so I can make time for her in the evenings after long shifts like that.

The rest of the week speeds by in a blur of kisses and missed conversations, because Meadow's schedule is insane.

And one of Tessa's baristas answers my job ad for the bartender gig, opening up three nights a week for me to be a good boyfriend. He starts the night before Halloween, and I use my newfound freedom to do even more work.

Tessa and I do a dress rehearsal of the street shut-down. Even without volunteers, we do a full roll-out in an hour, which is great.

"I had no doubt," she says when I walk her back to the bakery. "My Tarot card reading today was excellent."

"Cool."

She gives me a look like she's going to offer a reading, and I don't know if it's because of calendar, or what's going on with Meadow, but a part of me would take it.

Except she doesn't offer, so I mooch an end-of-day muffin off her and head back to the bar. I'm glad the new guy is serving drinks tonight because I'm not in a public mood.

I'm in a Meadow kind of mood, but she's working all night. She'll get off at seven tomorrow morning, sleep all day, and be good to go for the party.

Bas: I'm eating a Tessa muffin and thinking of you.
Meadow: That's the hottest thing I've ever heard. I'm picking at a slice of cold pizza.
Bas: Sexy.

She sends a selfie with the pizza slice, and it is sexy. Her hair is messy and her eyes are bright.

Bas: Yeah, you're fucking hot.
Meadow: Your turn.

I slouch back in my chair and turn on my camera. At the last second I drop my hand into my lap, my fingers surrounding the thick shape of my cock through my jeans.

She likes it.

Meadow: Hello, mister. I can't wait to crawl all over you tomorrow.
Bas: Right back at you. Tell me what your costume is.
Meadow: Nope. It's a surprise.
Bas: Tease.
Meadow: You can spank me for that later.

I grin at the screen.

Bas: I'd like that. Spanking, eh?
Meadow: If you like.
Bas: I like.

9

MEADOW

BAS WANTS TO SPANK ME.

I put it out there and he picked it up like a king. A gorgeous, kinky, thoughtful king.

We've had a week of kisses. A week of bodies pressed close and long, gorgeous hugs, but nothing more.

His plan to wait until after the party was a good one. The last month has been hectic at work, and now I'm looking at a lighter load for the next two weeks.

Lighter is relative for an obstetrician, but I'll have nights and weekends off.

And Bas will be able to focus on me. Us. This week has made me look at him differently. He's still the man I hunger for, but since admitting just how much I've wanted him, I've had to take a hard look at the reasons I'd talked myself into for not doing anything sooner—all my doubts about whether he would be able to commit, or if he was too flighty.

But the last week has shown me that he's restless, not reckless. For all his outwardly social behaviour, he's really an introvert and deep-down, quite cautious. I think it's possible that Bas has always held himself back—from relationships, from opportunities—to protect himself.

So I'm skipping as I leave the hospital on the morning of Halloween. Literally hopping with excitement, and I bounce right into Max Donovan in the parking lot.

In my defence, he steps out from behind a pillar just as I begin a twirl. He catches me and spins me away from him in one fluid motion. "You could be a figure skater for Halloween," he says with a chuckle.

"So could you." I catch my breath and wave my hand in apology. "Sorry about that."

"You are way too peppy for this early in the morning. Did you show up and realize you didn't need to stay?"

"Oh, I wish. No, I just got off a twenty-four-hour shift. But I've got party plans tonight." I wiggle my shoulders. "Bas's street party."

"Oh!" Max's eyebrows hit the roof. "That's great. I didn't realize you'd kept in touch with him."

Right. Because I'd told him it didn't work out, and then I definitely didn't tell him that I'd moved into the apartment over Bas's bar.

Max, like everyone else at the hospital, still thinks I live in my condo five blocks from here.

I mean, technically I do. I stay there once in a while when I don't want to drive all the way to Metcalfe.

Ugh. Happy vibe busted. I paste on a smile. "It's a long, weird story. We've become friends over time."

"That's fantastic. And have a good time tonight. I know a few people who are going, it sounds like it's quite the hot ticket event."

MAX WASN'T WRONG. By the time I wake up from the world's

longest post-call sleep, dusk is setting on Duke Street and there's a decent amount of noise coming from street-level. I wrap myself in my blanket and crawl over to the window to check it out.

I immediately smile, because Bas is in the middle of it all, a giant among men. Extra giant right now, because he's wearing some kind of fur vest that makes his already significant shoulders look positively massive as he points people in various directions.

When he turns around, I realize he's got a sword hanging off a thick leather belt, and are his pants leather, too?

I scramble higher on my knees, pressing my nose against the glass. No, they're black cargo pants, maybe. More practical, but still perfect for his sexy Viking costume.

I need to see his outfit up close. Which means I need to get dressed myself. Leotard first, then the garter belt and fishnet stockings, the ballet-styled boots, following by the tutu and finally the corset. A dirty, gritty ballerina. I twist my hair into a sophisticated twist with curls falling out of it, add a couple of sparkly spiders I found in the hospital gift shop, and swipe on a bit of lipgloss and mascara.

The last thing I want at the end of the night is to worry about taking off makeup before I bury my face in Bas's pillows. Or something.

Any answer to that hypothetical something is contraindicated for a full painted face. Sweat, happy tears, other bodily fluids…

I blush at myself in the mirror, add another dash of gloss, then make the spiders in my hair dance with a little wiggle.

I'm fully prepared to freeze my nipples off, because the corset just *barely* covers them—and without the leotard, that would be super dirty. But when I get downstairs and step outside, the super cool end-of-October air only nips at my nose for a second before I get a waft of something warmer.

"Bas thought of everything, didn't he?" Tessa asks, appearing from nowhere with a latte, which she hands over before waving at the portable heaters that are taking the chill off the air.

"Including this coffee for you, by the way. He said I should keep an eye out for you while he's fixing something down at the other end."

"Thanks." I don't miss her twinkling smile, but I'm not ready to answer any questions about Bas just yet, so I ignore that bit of her nosy neighour routine and admire her costume instead. "This is an awesome thing," I say, gesturing at her Wild West steampunk get-up. "Is your stall all set up?"

She curtsies. "Good to go, ready for people to arrive soon."

I crane my head to the side, but I can't see the big clock on Main Street.

Tessa reads my mind. "Half an hour to go until doors open. But all the stalls are set up, if you want to roam now before it gets busy."

"It's already busy," I murmur, taking a grateful sip of hot coffee.

"Go on," she urges.

I nod. I will. And then I realize—I'm nervous. "I will," I say out loud, more definitive now than it had sounded in my head. "I'll just take a minute to let it all soak in first."

She accepts that and turns away, bustling back across the road to the outdoor version of her shop.

At the far end of the street, I see Bas moving confidently. Solving problems. My breath catches in my throat as I take a first step, then a second, in his direction.

A vendor halfway down the street catches my eye. "Wicked boots," she says as I slow down to admire her chainmail work. Dragon scale gloves and heavy chain jewellery are unexpected additions to the table, and I slide my fingers over a dark blue metal choker. She grins. "That's a favourite with the kinky crowd."

My head jerks up. Does she mean *me*? How does she know? But she points behind me, and I turn around.

Bas wasn't kidding when he said it was going to dirty. There's a woman bent over a wooden structure. And since there's a guy lazily paddling her bottom, there's no other way to describe—that's a spanking bench.

So. Cool.

I turn back, grateful that it's gotten dark enough to hide my hot cheeks. "Pretty fun," I murmur.

"Oh yeah." She says it knowingly.

Bas is getting a grilling as soon as we're alone tonight. A thorough, filthy grilling, maybe with me over his lap and him giving me permission to quiz him point by point.

"How much for the choker?"

"Thirty."

I pull two twenties from the curve of my corset and hand them over. She makes change, then picks up the choker. "Do you want this packaged up, or are you adding it to your costume?"

"I'll wear it now, yeah." I take it from with thanks, but I don't put it on right away. I step into the street, looking for Bas. When I don't find him immediately, I make my way across the way to the booth for the Filthy Ottawa Social Club, as their sign proclaims.

The Spanking Bench Club, I call them in my head.

Or, the Tell Me More Club. Provided they have the same privacy rules as Fight Club.

Which reminds me that the prime minister's wife is going to arrive at some point, so until that happens, I can't distract my Viking.

Too much.

So I'll keep myself occupied.

"Are you interested in social nudity?" The man who'd previously been spanking his partner asked.

My mouth falls open.

He winks. "That's the official justification for our club. That and the creative artistic value inherent in roleplay."

"Oh. And the…unofficial justification?"

The soft bristle of fur slides against my skin as big, strong, arms wrap around me from behind, and Bas's voice growls in my ear. "Spanking, bondage, whipping. All manner of terrible things."

"Hi," I whisper, twisting around to see him.

He kisses me gently on the mouth. Then not-so-gently. "You found this booth."

"I did."

"Do you like it?"

"I don't know," I say at first, but that's not true. "Yes. It's… overwhelming but cool."

"Don't let Oliver scare you."

"I'm not scared." I turn back. "Hi Oliver. I'm Meadow."

Oliver holds out his hand. "A pleasure." Then he turns to greet someone new, and Bas guides me over to the spanking bench.

"Do you have one of these?" I ask, breathlessly.

He laughs. "No. I don't have any kinky furniture, but if you like it, I'll build you one by morning."

"I was…" I get as close to him as I can get and tip my head back to look at him. "I was thinking I'd like to be over your lap."

He growls and flexes his hands against my back. "Yes."

"How kinky are you?"

"As kinky as you want me to be? I want you to get off, I want to enjoy getting you off, I want to make you squirm, and control you a bit—if you'd like that."

"I'd *love* that."

"Have you ever played like this?"

"Not really. But I'm curious." I turn around to take it all in again, and the choker clatters in my hand. "Oh!" I hold it up. "I bought this. Just now."

One of his eyebrows curves high on his brow. "That's pretty kinky. And hot."

"Would you put it on me?"

He exhales and nods. "Absolutely."

After turning me around, he brushes a kiss on the top of my spine, then reaches around me and settles the chain against the fluttering pulse-point at the base of my neck. His fingers rub against my skin as he does up the latch, then settle on my shoulders.

"You look phenomenal," he murmurs in my ear, curving over my body. I can feel his gaze on the chain, on my chest and the curve of skin at the top of the leotard, even though I can't see his face. "I will be watching you all night, my sexy little ballerina. My gorgeous little one."

My heart swells as he turns me around.

"How does that sound?" he asks as he touches his fingertips to my chin.

I nod, wordlessly.

He shakes his head. "Tell me, Meadow."

"I like that," I whisper.

But before we can get into it further, there's a flurry of activity at the gates, and the Halloween street party is officially open.

I push up higher on my toes and kiss his jaw. "Find me later," I say, grinning broadly. I want this to be a roaring success for him. "I'm going to talk up the special brew at Duke & Main to everyone who looks thirsty."

"Meadow—" He grabs for me, but I'm out of reach now. Just for a few more hours. Then I'll be his little one until dawn.

"Go," I say, wiggling my fingers at him. "I bet Ellie Strong is going to be here any minute. Rumour has it she's hell on wheels. Better go and make sure she's well taken care of."

10

ELLIE

YES, THAT ELLIE! FROM PRIME MINISTER!

THIS IS THE FIRST GIRLS' night I have had in forever, and maximum fun depends on maintaining a low profile. My bodyguard, Corinne, found a minivan in the RCMP fleet—not something Gavin and I usually get transported in, although maybe we'll use it more as our family grows. It's perfect for traveling incognito, and surprisingly spacious and comfortable inside.

After some negotiation—where I told Gavin I would be fine with just Corinne and one more female officer—I agreed to a discreet back-up detail parked nearby.

My husband wasn't swayed by my suggestion that the bustling metropolis of Metcalfe might be perfectly safe for me to visit without any security at all. And then he played the "mother of my children" card and I capitulated. So when we park behind the bakery in town, Corinne tells me the other detail will be stationed on the other side of the street party, behind a bar called Duke & Main.

The back door of the bakery opens, and Corinne hustles us from the van and inside where she makes introductions.

"Ellie, this is Bas Absolom, the event organizer. Bas, Ellie Strong,"

I shake his outstretched hand. "Lovely to meet you, Bas. I appreciate the effort you've gone to so that my friends and I can blow off a little steam. I'd like you to meet Sasha, Beth, and Violet."

"Nice to meet you all," he says with a wide grin.

"There are goodies at all the stalls, so you'll need these," Bas says as he hands us each a small cotton bag with **Duke Street Trick or Treat** printed on them. "It's been lovely meeting you. I need to get back to the party. Enjoy yourselves and if there's anything you need, Corinne will let me know and I'll take care of it."

"Thank you," we all say in chorus, then dissolve into laughter. We all needed this, for sure.

Once we're alone, I take a good look at how my friends have dressed up. I was the last to be picked up, and the inside of the van was too dark to see much.

My best friend and former roommate has gone with a sexy twist on history. "Sasha, that costume is positively decadent. Cleopatra?"

"In the flesh. Left the snake at home, though."

"You really shouldn't talk about poor Tate, like that," Violet says with a wink. Then she shrugs out of her jacket, revealing more her costume. Not that there's much to see.

Sasha purrs. "Does Max know you're dressed up like a naughty little cheerleader?"

"He picked it out," Violet says. "Speaking of which..." She leans in. "Bas did a good job of pretending he doesn't know me, but within our cone of silence—" She wiggles her finger at us. We all know the drill.

Max and Violet are super kinky. We all are, in different ways, but they're the most free about it.

They get to be free about it.

"Cone of silence," I say breathlessly. I love kinky secrets.

Violet grins. "We've seen him at events. Max says he's a great Dom, really nice, excellent teacher."

Beth makes a happy sigh, and we all turn towards her.

She shrugs. "What? He has big hands. It's good to hear he knows how to use them. Don't worry, I'm happily taken with my sexy men."

Beth fell in love with two Mounties. And they both fell for her —and each other. They're adorable together.

As if she can read my mind, her cheeks turn pink, and she tugs the face part of her costume up and over her head, hiding her sweet embarrassment. "Enough of that," she says through the bright blue nylon.

"What exactly is your costume, anyway?" Violet asks. "I thought we were all doing the dirty thing." She tugs at the tiny cheer skirt.

Beth wiggles in the bright blue body stocking. "I'm not wearing anything underneath it, ladies. This is practically like streaking, in public, with my boss's wife by my side. And what could be dirtier than having your men cut their way in for some playtime to finish off the evening?"

"I take it back. That's wicked dirty. Ellie, meanwhile just looks all classy dressed up like a flapper."

"Hey," I protest in mock indignation. We all know I can't be photographed in bunny ears and a furry tail, as much as I might like that. There are rules one must follow when one is married to the prime minister. "Flappers can be dirty *and* classy."

Corinne is standing off to the side dressed like a sexy western sheriff—an excellent costume to include a very real weapon on her hip. She's obviously trying to hold in her amusement. She makes it easy for me to relax and just be me, and puts real effort into blending in without injecting herself into the situation. I appreciate that more than she can possibly know.

"Come on," Sasha says. "As much as it would be lovely to stand here and gab, there's a whole party waiting out there."

We make our way through the bakery, trick or treat bags firmly in hand. The other security officer is at the door waiting for us. She nods and heads out first, while Corinne brings up the rear.

The street is crowded, but it's not a complete crush. Not yet, anyway.

"Let's work our way up this side of the street, then come back down the other so we can stop for a drink or two before heading home," I suggest.

Everyone voices their agreement and we start off at the baker's stall. She's adorable in her steampunk outfit. Violet and I buy a muffin to eat on the way home and we move on.

"I want to check out the books," Violet says as we near the stall.

We stop to have a look, and Beth catches my eye and lifts a brow in question as we both notice there's a whole section on kink. I shake my head at her slightly. It's one thing to be here, but I can only imagine the fuss if it got out that the prime minister's wife and his assistant bought kinky sex books.

She nods and we go back to perusing the tamer offerings before continuing to the next stall. Here a local musician is selling CDs, and I happily buy one for us to listen to on the drive home. He recognizes me, which I expected, and we take a quick picture together.

"Do me a favour and don't post that to social media until I leave, okay?" I wink at him, and I think it'll work. Everyone likes a conspiratorial whisper and being in on a secret with a VIP.

It's still hard to think of myself as that, even after two years of being in Gavin's life and more than a year of marriage. Most of the time, I'm still Ellie Montague, a PhD student constantly negotiating another six months for her dissertation.

But then there's a red carpet event, or an important announcement, or—shudder—an election, like the one coming next year. And then I'm very much Mrs. Gavin Strong, a part of his public image and entirely up for critique.

We collect candy at a few more stalls. My favourite is a costume shop stall. They have the most incredible masks, and the proprietor is wearing an ornate plague mask with an elongated beak nose.

As part of his stall he has a gorgeous human-sized birdcage, at least ten feet tall, with creaky door that swings easily on its hinges when I touch it. "Would you like to try it out?" the man in the plague mask says, and oh, yes, I would.

But I can't.

Always aware of the optics.

"Maybe Sasha?" I suggest, turning to my friends. My bestie happily complies, dancing her way into the cage. We howl as I close her in, the creak of the door adding to the whole ambience.

Beth snaps our picture with my phone, then another further away. "For your personal reference, should you want to have a cage made," she whispers when she hands it back.

I adore my friends. I whisper my thanks back.

Then it's on to the next stall, and the one after that. "Trick or treat!" we call out, collecting candy in our bags.

It takes more than an hour to complete the loop. When we pass the Filthy Ottawa Social Club, Beth and I leave Sasha and Violet to play on the spanking bench together, and we go on ahead to the bar.

"Did you have fun?" I ask Sasha when they finally join us. "We ordered a round of the signature cocktails, they should be here soon."

"Oh yeah, spanking was *amazing*."

Violet's cheeks are pink. "She's a natural. Maybe Tate's bottom doesn't know what's coming?"

"Maybe," Sasha murmurs. "Although Tate's bottom likes most things that I do to it, so…he'll be game."

"You mean…" I clear my throat and look around. "Not here."

From behind me, Corinne is laughing. I don't blame her.

"No, not here," Beth says smoothly. "But in the van."

I nod. "Oh yes. In the van. One hundred percent."

Sasha beams. Of course she wants to show off her *I-know-where-my-man's-prostate-is* skills. She's a freak.

We all are.

It's wonderful.

"Ladies," a booming voice says above us. "I have your drinks."

We look up as one at Bas, who serves us four shimmering drinks, each one a slightly different opalescence. Pinks, blues, oranges, and reds all swirl together with some kind of edible sparkle dust scattered over the surface.

"To Halloween," Sasha says, lifting her glass.

I lift mine. "And to Bas, because this has been some much needed fun."

"To Bas!" we all cry out, our glasses tinkling.

He winks. "And with that, I'll leave you be. I have a woman to find."

"Ohhhh," Beth and Sasha say.

"Awwww," Violet and I say.

And then it's Bas Absalom's turn to blush.

11

BAS

I FIND Meadow talking to Oliver. He's playing with a pile of neatly bound rope bundles, and she's all over him in a sweet, innocent, eager rope bunny kind of way.

That bodes well for me. So well.

I dodge around a man on stilts and join them. "Having fun?"

She beams at me. "Oliver offered to let me tie him up! Isn't that sweet?"

"Adorable. Do you want to?"

She shakes her head. "Not really. But his demonstration sounds neat."

Oliver is a mutual friend of mine and Corinne's. He knows the drill. Once our VIP guest leaves, he can get his kink on more freely, and I've secured a safe suspension tether point on the front of Duke & Main.

When I installed it earlier this week, I wondered if I was going overboard for a single-use public performance. But two hours into this street party, I'm sure I'll do it again next year. The theatrical magic happening around us right now is more than I ever imagined—and I've got a pretty robust imagination for magical fantasy.

Meadow catches my eye and I hold my arm out so she can fold into my side.

"What are you thinking?" she asks quietly.

"Wondering if we've got the right balance of music to stall chatter."

"Notes for next year?"

I look down at her. "How'd you know?"

She thinks about it for a moment. "Something's shifted. I don't know, I just knew."

Because she sees me and gets me. I kiss the top of her head. "Yeah. Notes for next year."

She hugs me tight. "Good."

"How are you doing? Not tired?"

"Nope. I've got big plans later, so I'm well-caffeinated."

That makes me laugh. Big plans. "I've got plans, too."

"Excellent," she whispers. "Because my plans are just to let you do whatever you want."

Ah, fuck. Now I want this magical street party to be over right now, and we've still got a few hours to go. "Go on, little one. Find something to distract yourself with for a bit."

She does a glorious pirouette and laughs. "Later, Viking."

I growl.

THE NEXT TIME I find her, she's watching Oliver string up a volunteer in front of my bar. She leans against my chest and I don't offer any commentary. She doesn't ask for any. It's all wide-eyed wonder and raw appreciation.

When he finally releases his willing victim, Meadow applauds and lets out an excited whoop. Then she sighs as Oliver hugs the rope bottom, holding them close for a moment.

"That was lovely. I've never seen aftercare in person," she says once the crowd disperses.

"You know about aftercare." I tug her into the shadows between two buildings.

"I know a lot of things. I know what I want, and what I might like. What I want to try." She walks her fingers up my chest, then strokes them over my jaw. "I'm not the vanilla girl you thought I was."

"I'm figuring that out."

"But tonight, I just want you." Her words light me on fire, and I crush my mouth against hers.

She climbs up my body, a nimble little bunny, and I press her back against the brick wall with care.

We kiss until we're both out of breath and my cock is rock hard. Then I hold her in place and just…breathe. Ragged inhales and slow, deliberate exhales.

"One more hour," she whispers.

Before I can answer her, something vibrates between us.

She laughs weakly. "And…my pager just went off. It'll be a consult call, but I gotta go check."

I kiss her again, tasting the corner of her mouth. Someone did some trick-or-treating, because she tastes like candy even after all our kissing.

"Meet me in my apartment when you're done cleaning up?"

I pat her hip and set her down. "Take off the leotard before you answer the door." My hands linger on her skin. "The rest of the costume…that's up to you."

Even in the dark, I can see her react.

And my dick throbs.

IT'S NEARLY midnight by the time I knock on her door. There's no answer at first. Maybe she's on the phone still, maybe she fell asleep.

Maybe I'm this is the Cinderella of fantasy fuck stories and I don't get to sleep with Meadow after all.

But then there's a flurry of steps and the door swings open, and all my fears disappear.

She's still in costume. No leotard. Her breasts threaten to spill over the top of the corset and her tutu doesn't quite cover the fact that she's not wearing any panties.

"Bas," she breathes. "I was just—"

I sweep her into my arms and move forward into the apartment, the door shutting hard behind me.

We should talk.

We will talk.

She bites my lower lip.

Yeah, talk will happen very soon. We just need to do something else first—fuck, hard and fast. Nothing that requires negotiation.

But it's been a week of anticipation.

"No more waiting," Meadow whispers as she slides her hands under my fur vest. "Please. Pillage my village, Bas."

I howl, because this woman is fucking funny. Sweet and hot and funny, and I'm overthinking everything. Effortlessly, I pick her up, and she wraps her thighs around my waist. Her legs are soft and warm under my touch.

That's where I'm starting, just as soon as I can get her to a horizontal surface. She pushes my vest off in her doorway, and after I dump her unceremoniously on the bed, I make short work of my belt and boots.

Her boots are gone, too, her fishnet legs soft and touchable and very spreadable.

I crawl after her and wrap my hands over her knees. "May I?"

"Anything," she murmurs, stretching out.

"Spread these for me. Show me how beautiful you are."

Her thighs tremble beneath my touch, but she doesn't hesitate. Her legs slide apart and I crawl closer, needing to catch that first scent of her. See the glisten, and then, once she starts squirming, lean in for a first taste.

She's perfect. Coppery sweet, slick and generous in her arousal. I start gently, but she likes firm flicks of my tongue and hard pulls on her clit. I suck on her until her thighs wrap hard around my head and her pussy throbs in a pulsing orgasm.

When she falls back on the bed, languid and sexy, I stand again and get rid of my cargo pants—keeping one of the condoms I'd pocketed earlier.

"You want to fuck me like this?" She asks, wiggling her tutu skirt.

Yes. That way, every way. "Roll over," I demand. "Show me the back of this corset."

She flips onto her front, then takes her time pushing up onto all fours, ass first. The pale white swells of her bottom, the darker line between her cheeks, and then, demanding to be fucked, the swollen folds of her pussy present themselves.

Who cares about the fucking corset?

12

MEADOW

I'm hot all over and slick between my legs. I'm wanton and desperate and if Bas doesn't fuck me soon, I'm going to tackle him to the bed and do it myself.

But I don't have to take over, because his hands are on my hips and then everything changes. Every nerve in my body tingles differently when he's touching me, when he's firm—ah, and rough, that's good too. The hard bite of his fingers into the curve of my flesh makes me bow my head, search for a pillow to bury my screams in.

"You like that, little one? My hands on you?"

I groan and nod, and his next press is on my back, pushing the air out of my lungs. Ah, again. I twist my head to the side so he can see my smile.

His fingers rake up my back, over the lacing on the corset, and tangle hard in my hair. A tug. Another smile.

"Like that, too?"

"Mmm."

"I'm going to fuck you now." A statement. A promise. A threat, if I drift into fantasy land. So good.

"Please…"

He's so big, he can do it while he's got his hand tangled in my hair, holding me down. He notches his cock against my wet, slick hole and pushes inside. Hard. Rough. Perfect in its stretch, amazing in its depth. He takes up space inside me I didn't know I had to give, and he lights it up with magic.

The street fair is long gone now, but I can still hear the music, the laughter, the kinky delight.

Arching my back, I push back against him, bringing him deeper into my body. All the way in, until his body is pressed hard against mine.

I ache and feel good—so good—at the same time. Like I'm going to have to get used to having him buried in me, and I kind of don't want to forget the shock of his size.

And then he starts moving. Slowly at first, dragging his solid length out of me and pushing back in. More magic, more shock.

"So good," I tell him, and my voice doesn't even sound like me. I sound better. Like Meadow+, now full of perfect cock. I laugh a little, and it fades into a happy sigh.

"Yeah?"

"Oh, Bas…"

"That's what I like to hear. You want more, little one?" His hands are on my hips now, he's let go of my hair and he's holding on to my sides, his fingers tangled around the garter belt straps, like I should be warned of impending thrusts.

"More."

His next thrust is harder, and the one after that faster. I close my eyes and bury my face in the bed, giving myself over to the sensations.

His hands. His cock. The wet slap and the thick drag against nerves.

His sounds.

The flex of his body behind me, and then, when he starts to fumble, on top of me. He pushes forward, almost crushing me— yes, please, be heavy—but then he pulls out—no!—and flips me over. It's just a few seconds but I ache at the loss of him. I reach for his slick, condom-covered cock and bring it back to my cunt, fitting us together as he tumbles down.

We move as one. Kissing, fucking. My costume is in the way a bit but it doesn't matter. I'm close now, everything tight and needy. Rub, push, rock, fuck.

When I come, it's an explosion. And even as my climax rockets through me, I can feel Bas shudder, then long, heavy pulses deep inside me. I hear him, too. New sounds. A guttural gasp of relief, then something else.

My name, over and over again, breathed against my neck, where he's buried his face.

"Meadow, oh, Meadow, fuck yeah, Meadow…"

It's beautiful. I press my hand to his head and hold him. In the last week, he's held me over and over again. Now it's my turn to soothe the giant, and something wonderful slips into place inside me.

We lie like that longer than we should when there's a condom to deal with, but it's fine as he pulls away. He disappears into my bathroom for a moment, then returns. "Do you need to pee?"

I grin. "Yeah, be a second."

When I catch sight of myself in the mirror, I laugh. The corset is sideways, the tutu is ripped—but repairable. And I'm very glad I didn't wear more makeup, because the mascara is streaked. I quickly wipe that away, then take care of business and rejoin him on the bed.

"So, funny story," he says as he unlaces my corset, his fingers tickling my skin with each pulling release.

I shiver. "Mmm?"

"I saw someone I wasn't expecting to see tonight."

I guard myself. "An ex?"

"God, no. This wouldn't be the time for that kind of a share."

"Right. But I'd be cool with it. I mean, sharing is good."

He chuckles under his breath and kisses my bare shoulder.

"You wouldn't be cool with it. You're adorably possessive and that's just fine with me. No, I saw the wife of a friend. Well, I guess she's an acquaintance, too, although I know Max more than Violet."

I freeze. Max's wife was here tonight? He hadn't said she'd be here. But Max wasn't a sharer. And we aren't really that close, other than him knowing the stupid secrets I blurt out in staff meetings.

"Max Donovan?"

"Do you know him? He's a doctor, too, so I thought you might. Small world."

"Very," I murmur. "So why is that a funny story?"

"Well, what happens in the dungeon usually stays in the dungeon, but I also like to prepare partners in advance—full disclosure and all that. Honesty is the best policy."

"Max goes to dungeons?" I squeak it, and it comes out wrong. I twist awkwardly, trying to get Bas to see my face. Like I'm not judging that—at all. "That's cool. Super fine."

Bas gives me a gentle smile. "And we don't ever have to do that if you don't want to."

"That's not what I'm saying. Dungeons sound…well, they sound made-up, to be honest. Like something out of a book or a movie, not like real things that people I work with actually go to. Although now that you've said that, it explains a few things. A lot of things. What do you mean his wife was here tonight and it's funny?" My words are spilling fast now, total stream of consciousness.

Bas takes my hands. "Calm down. She's good friends with Ellie Strong. It was a girls' night out thing."

I'd seen the PM's wife from a distance. I'd assumed all the women with her were bodyguards or something. "Right."

"And it's just that I realized our worlds might collide, and I should be upfront."

Oh God, I'm going to throw up. "About that."

"Yeah?"

I wince. "So a while ago, you had a conversation with Max. I don't know exactly what it was about, but he brought up a doctor friend of his he thought you might like to meet. And you asked for her number. Max didn't want to overshare, so he said—"

Bas's face freezes granite hard. His mouth barely moves. "He said he'd give my number to her instead. I never heard from her."

"Because I came in person," I whisper. "To introduce myself. There was another woman, though, you called her lovely, and then you asked if I was here to see the apartment."

"You weren't here for that."

"No."

"You rented this place, though."

"I did."

"You didn't need an apartment?" He blinks at me, then his face falls. "Fucking hell, Meadow, do you have another place close to the hospital?"

Panic screams through every cell in my body. "Bas, it's complicated."

"I bet it's fucking complicated, Jesus Christ." He shoves off the bed and grabs at his clothes. "Don't—I mean, what the *fuck*—were you ever going to tell me?"

"I rent out my condo," I say miserably. "To AirBnB people. I only sleep there if I'm on shift and it happens to be vacant. This is where I live now."

"Because you couldn't be up front with me."

When it says it like that, it sounds exactly as terrible as it is. "Bas—"

"Don't." He shakes his head as he yanks on his pants. "Just… don't."

And then he leaves. All my words die on my tongue, and all my hopes disintegrate in his wake as he storms out.

1 3

BAS

I GET AS FAR as the street before I realize I've fucked up. The light is still on in the bakery across the way, so I knock on the door.

Tessa opens the door, yawning as she swings it open. "I thought you'd gone off to bed."

"Same to you."

She gestures at the bright kitchen behind her. "Gotta get the baking done for tomorrow—or later today, really. I've got a part-timer coming in to work for me at five, so I just need to stay up until then."

"Ah." I pace around the dim space in front of the empty display. "Got any leftover muffins from tonight?"

"Nope." She smiles broadly. "Totally sold out. But if you wait five minutes, I can give you fresh ones straight out of the oven."

Five minutes sounds like a lifetime, but I don't want to return empty handed and it would take longer to drive into the city for flowers.

Also, I have no fucking clue if Meadow likes cut flowers. But she loves muffins. She picks them apart, tiny bite by tiny bite, and licks her fingers clean when she's done eating them.

Muffins are a glorious thing.

And a decent place to start my apology, once I work out my messed up thoughts.

"Were you happy with tonight?" Tessa asks. "Pretty cool that Ellie Strong came, eh?"

"Very." I clear my throat. "Yeah, it was a roaring success. We'll have to do it again next year."

"Count me in. I had a couple of people say they'll drive out on the weekend to pick up muffins. If that catches on, it'll be totally worth it."

"You should do more of a brunch offering on the weekend," I say, looking out the window at the dark, quiet street.

She laughs from the kitchen. "At my three tables? No, I want customers to come and go. In and out. If anyone should do a fancy farm-to-table brunch, it's you. Your space is perfect for it."

I'm looking across at my bar, and I hear her words, but I don't really hear them. Not at first.

Then they sink in, and I slowly turn around.

"No," I say, heading back toward her. "I shouldn't. I'm not a chef. But we could partner on it. My space, my drinks, your muffins, and we hire a chef. I don't want to manage another venture, but I'm happy to donate the space and provide the cocktails. You're up early anyway. You can oversee the food prep, the menu design."

She blinks at me. "Just like that?"

I shrug. "Meadow really likes your muffins."

She winks. "And you really like Meadow."

Was it that fucking obvious to everyone who isn't me and Meadow? "Yeah, I do."

"Are these for her?" She gestures to the tray she's just pulled out of the oven.

I nod.

She tuts her tongue against her teeth and shakes her head. "Middle of the night muffins for your woman. Must have been something."

The something is that I wasn't clear enough that she is my woman, no matter what. I got mad and I left without saying why. Without explaining.

I'll fix that.

"Yeah, it was something all right."

She carefully sets four muffins in a cardboard carryout box, then sprinkles a couple of sugared flower petals across the top before closing it up. "Make it right, Bas. I like the way your mind works when she's inspiring you."

I take the box gratefully. "Me, too."

I make it as far as the door before I turn around. "Tessa?"

"Yeah?"

"Does your Tarot deck say anything about this moment?"

She grins. "You sure you want to know?"

I nod. I do.

She pulls it out from behind the counter and carefully hands it over. "Shuffle this, and as you do that, think of your question. The more specific the better. Then take one, and I'll read it for you."

I take the cards and rifle them. I'm not as sure as I should be on this question, but I know my energy. I know myself.

I pull a card from the middle and hand it over.

Tessa grins as soon as she looks at it. "Oh, Bas, the cards never lie." She flips it over so I can see it, not that I know what they mean. "This is the Page of Swords, and he is so you. Stubborn, energetic, an excellent negotiator. But he can also mean that you've got a lot of decisions to make, and quickly. If you are looking for a yes or no answer to a question, the Page of Swords is a clue that you're smart and capable, and if you've settled whatever has held you back in the past, going forward you should say yes." She pauses. "I don't want to assume this is Meadow related, but hell, man, say yes."

I grin and set the rest of the deck on the counter. "Have no fear, Tessa."

When Meadow answers the door, she's no longer wearing the remnants of her costume. Instead, she's changed into an over-size t-shirt.

Dropping the box of muffins on the small table by the door, I crowd Meadow up against the wall, her hands splayed against my chest.

"Stop it, Bas." She shoves at me, but I'm ten times bigger than her. I don't move. She glares at me. "What are you doing?"

"Having the rest of a conversation."

"It's not nice to hold a girl against the wall, you know."

"I'm not a nice man."

"That's a lie."

"It's the truth. I didn't listen to you. And now I'm pinning you against a wall. What would you call that?"

"You're not a nice man," she whispers, and her pupils dilate.

I shake my head. "I'm a bastard in so many ways. But you make me nice. And if you've got secrets, so do I. I thought you were too good for me. Too kind, too sweet. Not dirty enough."

She blushes, and stupid me would have thought that proved my point, but I'm wide awake to all the different ways Meadow is delightfully filthy now. "I'm pretty dirty," she says softly, and it's the fucking hottest thing I've ever heard.

"Yeah you are. So the question now is, what do you want to do next?"

She licks her lips. "I lied to you."

My craven impulses could not have been more on point. "Do you want to be punished for that?"

A soft, sweet whimper slides across her lips. "Would that be okay?"

Fucking hell. I grin broadly. "Yeah, baby. That would be more than okay."

"Do you… I mean, how would you…"

I lean all the way in, closing the space between us to nothing but dark heat. "I've got all sorts of ideas, little one. Six months of fantasies to make up for. Six months of secrets to punish you for. But I think it would be a reward to tell you what *I* want to do. That would be too easy. Too nice. So I want to make you say it. Tell me what you think should happen. Be brave, Meadow. Tell me. Where do you want to begin? What did you think the first time you saw me?"

"Your hands," she pants. "They're what I noticed first."

"How big they are?"

"Yes." It's a whisper now. Her voice is shaking, and that gets to me. Right in the middle of my selfish chest.

"What did you want, Meadow? Tell me. Anything."

"I wanted you to spank me."

"Right from the very beginning?"

"Yes."

"And you kept that from me?"

Her voice breaks. "Y-es."

"Why?"

"Because you were always…"

"With someone else?" That's not really true, though. There were breaks. "How many women have I been with in the last six months?"

Her face twists as she thinks. "A few."

"For how long?"

She whimpers. "Not long."

"None of them were you, little one."

She cries out now, and it hurts me. But I push on.

"I wanted you, too. Don't you know that now? And you were so tangled up in your secrets that you couldn't see it."

Her eyes squeeze shut and she nods. Slowly, carefully, I cover her wrists with my hands. I squeeze, and she shudders. "I'll spank you tonight, then. We'll start there. But I'll want more. A lot more."

She gasps, and another jolt of need zaps through me.

"Will you want more, too?" I know the answer, though. I can

feel her pulse racing against my grip, see her body slowly writhing against me.

"Yes," she whispers. "All of it. Anything."

I should take her back to bed. Fuck her senseless. Spank her first, of course. Then fuck her red bottom until she comes on my cock in a slippery mess.

Except now we've headed in a different direction, one with rules. I clear my throat. "We need to discuss limits."

"Okay." A breathy, perfect response.

I grin down at her. "What are yours?"

She blinks. "I don't know."

That trips me up. "Pardon?"

She shrugs, and her too-big t-shirt slides dangerously low on her chest. I could get completely distracted by her freckles.

I want to count every single dot on her body.

And I will, but later. First, we need to get some boundaries clearly set out so I don't fucking break her perfect little self.

"I can't imagine anything I wouldn't let you do to me," she whispers.

I growl. For real, out loud, I make a feral noise that's half outrage, because what the fuck, that's not okay. And half, holy fuck, because it's also everything I've ever dreamed of. "That's fucking hot," I say, my voice full of grit and want. And control. Somehow, I hold the fuck onto that. "But everyone has limits."

"Really?" she asks. "Because I've thought about, like, everything, and if you're doing it, it sounds awesome."

I'm pretty sure my control is about to go out the fucking window. "Tell me."

"I want you to fuck me. Like, rough. Hard. Out of control. Pull my hair, spank me, even put your hand around my throat. Use... things on me. Uh...ropes sound cool." She inhales quickly. "Tie me to a fucking chair, and force your big, fat cock into my wet, little mouth."

Sweet, glorious Meadow. I step back so she can see me fully, and I drag her hands down to press against my cock, hard and heavy in my jeans. "That was very brave," I tell her. "And an excellent list." Then I catch her by her waist and swing her into the air. I grunt as she squeaks in protest. "Get your hot little ass into my lap for the rest of this conversation."

She buries her face into my neck, her hair bouncing against my face. She smells like vanilla.

Of course I thought she was too pure for my depraved brand of filth.

And of course I was wrong.

"You deserve a redo on this," I say as I move us to the couch in front of the fireplace. "On the whole God damn thing. You deserve for me to say something when we first met. I didn't do that."

"I didn't either."

"Good. We're both on the same equal footing. I've heard that's important in relationships."

I sit down and arrange her in my lap so I can see her face. "I want to do everything you said. I like pushing my partners a little bit out of their mind, freeing them to feel a blissful combination of nothing and everything. But that line is different for everyone, and sometimes different at any given time. I have a hard limit on blood play, for example."

Her eyes go wide. "That's a limit for me, too, I guess."

"See?"

"I know you have more experience with this than I do," she murmurs, her cheeks turning pink. "I guess I just got excited."

"I like excited. And I don't want to bog us down with rules. Sex doesn't need to follow any kind of script. But talking about it can be hot. It can also be…" I think back to earlier, how I hustled out of her bed. "Vulnerable," I admit. "Like before. I got my back up about you keeping stuff from me. But you had your reasons, and the more I think about that, the more I understand. I want to understand, anyway."

"There's nothing more to it," she says, her voice small. "I made a rash decision in the moment, and then hid it as we became friends. After a while, I resigned myself to just being friends, and it didn't matter."

"What about the last week?"

She makes a small, helpless sound, and her eyes well up. "I wanted tonight, too. The kinky street party, the dirty costume. You didn't see me like that. You thought I was adorable."

Ah, fuck me. "I see what I did there, little one. I'm sorry for that."

"So we both have things to make up for," she says softly.

I cup her face in my hand. "Yeah."

The smile she gives me is beyond sweet. It's perfect. And then —because she's also filthy—she wiggles her ass in my lap.

"Are we done talking again, Meadow? Do you want me to take you over my knee?" I say it as evenly as I can. The answer might be no.

She nods and wiggles again, and yes, I'm done talking.

And that promised spanking might just be what we both need right now.

I flip her over my knee and slide the t-shirt up over her curvy bottom. Her skin is so pale, a perfect canvas. I rub my palm over one cheek, squeezing and tapping until it pinkens. She squirms beautifully in my lap, letting out adorable little mewling noises and my already aching cock is straining against my jeans, eager to be inside her tight little body again.

I continue peppering her skin with light smacks, and once I'm satisfied her ass is properly warmed up, I lay down my first real strike.

She tilts her hips forward into my thigh as she releases a long, low moan.

As I mark her entire bottom with my palm, she continues to rock against my leg.

I've spanked people before. I've played it bossy, I've let it be pure sex. It's never been quite like this before. Both punishment and redemption, erotic and free and controlled all at the same time.

"Do you want to come, little one?" I ask.

"Oh God, yes, please."

I scoop her up and carry her to the bedroom where I peel her shirt up and off her delectable little body. She gives me a silly, half-buzzy smile as I step back to undress again.

This time, I won't be getting dressed again until tomorrow.

Tonight, I want to feel her skin against mine all night long. I want to fuck her senseless and make her come so hard she sees stars. I want to fall into a deep, happy sleep with her wrapped in my arms. And in the morning, we'll keep talking.

There's so much still to discover.

No more secrets.

When I pull my shirt over my head, I realize I'm grinning, too. Maybe we're both a bit spun-out on this whirlwind of a night.

"Hey," she says, giggling.

"Do something for me," I say quietly as I palm another condom and sit on the edge of the bed. "Do one of those ballet pirouette things, little one. I want a good look."

Pleasure blooms over her face, and she lifts up onto her toes, turning slowly, letting me drink in the beauty that is mine to touch and tease and torment.

And love.

Halfway through her second revolution I drag her onto the bed because I'm naked and all out of patience.

Crawling between her legs, I rise up big and tall, and make a show of rolling on the condom.

"You know what I thought when I saw you this evening in your costume? You looked like a king," she says softly. "I like that. My king. You look pretty regal right now, in a brutish, fuck-me kind of way."

"I'll be whatever you want," I tell her with a growl as I cover her body with mine. I lace my fingers with hers and slide our hands above her head. I push my cock deep inside her as I press my lips to hers. She opens to me, and I lick into her mouth, fucking it with my tongue.

I'll be her king. She can be my queen. And my little one. My sweet, adorable, sexy Meadow.

EPILOGUE

MEADOW

Another six months later

IT'S BEEN A LONG, hard day that ended with an emergency C-section that came so heartbreakingly close to tragedy. And all I want when I get home is a long, hot bath with a glass of wine and a good book with a happy ending.

Bas leans over the bar and gives me a toe curling kiss. "Looks like you've had a rough day."

"Little bit."

"You want to talk about it?"

"I was thinking of taking a hot bath and forgetting it," I admit.

He grins. "Fair enough. Did you get my text?"

I shake my head and pull out my phone, which I'd shoved in my bag when I left the hospital. I read the message in front of him.

Bas: I found something fun when I was reorganizing a closet. If you're up for it, I want to play tonight.

I lift my head, suddenly less weary. Playtime sounds like an even better distraction. "Yes, please."

He brushes his fingers over my jaw. "Good girl. I'll make sure you get a bath at the end of the night, don't worry. Head on up and get changed. I'll be there in a few minutes."

When I walk into our bedroom, I see my Halloween costume lying on the bed—without the leotard this time—with a big note pinned to it that says *Put this on, then go immediately to the playroom.*

The playroom. I giggle and do a happy dance.

Our apartment is really both of the apartments above the bar, with the wall knocked out in between. My old bedroom is at one end, this room is at the other—and since Bas had the bigger bed, this is the one we kept as a sleeping space.

The other room is now kink-central, a glorious space I love spending time in.

And it's soundproof, because my man is as practical as he is sexy.

I quickly strip out of my clothes, and only when I'm fully naked, do I start dressing. First with the garter belt, then I roll on each black fishnet stocking. Once they're attached, I step into the short tulle skirt then fasten myself in the corset, adjusting my boobs so my nipples poke out the top. Finally, I slide my feet into the ballet boots and lace them up.

So cute.

I try not to think about what Bas could have in mind for tonight beyond the fact that it will result in me being reduced to a puddle of thoroughly satisfied woman in his arms.

Bas is waiting for me in the playroom when I arrive. He's wearing well-worn distressed blue jeans, my favourite, a black t-shirt that shows off every muscle, and an evil grin.

"You look lovely, little one. I want you over there," he says pointing to my right. There on the wall is a full-length mirror and what appears to be a barre. When did he install that?

"Today," he answers. Of course he knew exactly what I was thinking.

Am I that predictable?

"Why?"

"Because a long time ago, you loved dance. And the thought of watching you practice turns me on. Win-win." He cocks an eyebrow and nods his head towards the barre. "Stretch and warm up like you would at a ballet class."

Oh. Okay, that's hot. Yes, please. But as a point of order, I'm totally in the wrong shoes. "To do that, I'd need to change into proper footwear. If you prefer the boots, I can make them work."

"I prefer the boots, but not if they could cause you injury, little one."

I wink. "I can make the boots work. Tomorrow, though, I'm totally ordering slippers."

His eyes darken in appreciation. "Please do."

I approach the barre solemnly, everything coming back. It doesn't matter that I'm no longer a hundred pounds soaking wet and I've got more curves than I used to for all of these poses.

Tonight, those curves are not going to be a problem. I don't need to push myself to the limit, I don't need to break my body to get this right. A shiver runs through me. I can just do what I want, and Bas is going to watch. It is a win-win, he's right.

I choose a combination of positions to both stretch and warm up my muscles. I like this a lot. It's fun to have his eyes on me, and it has the bonus of actually getting my body ready for whatever it is that Bas has planned. It's also surprisingly relaxing to move my body like this after a long day of tight, controlled work. And I get to tease him mercilessly by not quite showing off my assets.

I know that's working from the not-quite-silent sounds he makes as I stretch my limbs long and tall and low, giving him peeks that don't last nearly long enough.

On the third low sweep of my hand, his growl is a warning. I lift my head and smile angelically. His jaw flexes and he crooks his finger. "I think that's quite enough, little one. Come over here and bend over, legs spread as wide as you can with your palms on the floor."

I straighten up and walk as delicately as I can manage.

Once I'm in position, he circles around me and trails a finger down my spine. "Beautiful."

I tremble as his touch pauses at the tulle skirt, then lifts. When it returns, it's between my legs. Rude and promising at the same time. I gasp as his fingers dip into my slippery heat. Already wet. Already aching.

Then he slides one digit back to my tiniest hole and circles it. I shiver. Yes, please.

But it's not going to be that easy.

"On second thoughts…" His touch disappears. "Put your ankle up on the barre and bend over and rest your wrist on it."

After I return to the barre, he pulls a long pink ribbon from his back pocket, because he was prepared for this, clearly, and binds my wrist and ankle to the wood, tying the ribbon off in a big bow.

"Don't move."

As if.

I watch him in the mirror as he opens the middle drawer of the cabinet against the adjacent wall and pulls out lube and *his* favourite buttplug. The one that has four bulges, each bigger than the last. The one that I have a love-hate relationship with. I hate it because it's always so hard to take that last bulge, but love it because it means Bas is going make my world explode in the best possible way.

Flipping open the lid on the lube, he squirts a generous amount on the top of the plug, then swirls it down and around until he reaches the third bulge, then sets the bottle on top of the cabinet.

He catches me watching in the mirror and smiles. "Do you want to come, little one?"

"Yes, please."

He doesn't respond until he's behind me again.

"You're going to have to work for it," he says as he presses the tip of the plug against my back hole.

That first bulge always slides in so easily.

Deceitful little fucker.

The second is only a little stretch.

Number three creates a bit of a burn, but Bas is a firm believer in too much lube is almost enough, so it's bearable.

Sucking in a deep breath, I close my eyes and prepare to take the last one. As the pressure increases, I exhale slowly. Normally, I'd push into it, but my current predicament makes that impossible. I can't hold back the groan when the last bulge finally pops through.

Bas leans over my back, grinding his erection against the base of the plug as he pinches one of my nipples and tugs that breast further out of the corset. My clit throbs.

"Good girl," he whispers against my ear, repeating the gesture on the other breast before cupping both of them and giving me a good, hard squeeze.

Those words always send a warm shiver down my spine. The added nip at my earlobe along with another hard tweak of my nipples send me straight to my happy place.

I take a deep breath and focus the last bit of my non-buzzy conscious thoughts on staying upright. My standing leg is shaking. All of me is shaking.

The tell-tale buzz of a vibrator penetrates my consciousness just before it touches my clit. But it doesn't stay there long. Bas takes the vibe away just as I think I could come like this. Apparently, when he said I have to work for it, he meant more than just the battle of the bulges.

I don't know how much I'm going to be able to withstand. Normally, when he edges me, I'm not so precariously situated.

Breathe, Meadow. Stay standing.

The vibrator returns, and I want nothing more than to come, even though I know that's not going to happen. Which probably makes me want it even more.

I whine when he takes it away again. It's such evil torture.

"Patience, little one."

Translation: Whine again and I'll take even longer to make you come. So I quiet my mind and my mouth and let him torture me because it makes us both happy.

It feels like forever and a million lost orgasms when Bas finally unties my ankle and wrist. I'm buzzing hard and a lovely mess of scrambled feelings. He drapes the ribbons over the barre, then turns to me. Cupping my chin, he kisses me long and slow, stoking my already burning need. "Very good. You took that beautifully. Thank you."

I smile as he strokes his hands over my outfit. "This was a fun surprise."

"I like to remember that night."

"Me, too," I say softly.

He stops in front of me and strokes my cheek. "But it's time for us to be naked now, yes?"

I nod. "Please."

He strips me out of the corset first, then the skirt. He stops there and looks down at my fishnet clad legs. Through his jeans, I can see his erection straining. "Leave the stockings and boots on. Go lie on the bed on your back, arms above your head."

I hurry across the room, not bothering to hide my eagerness. I don't think I could ever play it cool, but definitely not with a giant plug in my ass and my thighs slick with anticipation. I want every orgasm Bas has to offer, and I want them as soon as he's willing to give them.

As soon as I'm still on the bed, Bas approaches. "You were very patient," he says with a warm smile. "Are you ready to come for me?"

"Yes," I whisper.

He pulls the ribbon from behind his back—when did he grab it?—and the vibrator, too. "Catch," he says, lobbing the latter gently beside me on the bed.

I don't move, and he chuckles.

"So well behaved," he murmurs, leaning over me. He sears my mouth with a kiss before picking up the vibrator and pressing it into my hand. "I was going to tie you up again here, but now I have a better idea. Use this on yourself. Don't come, just get close."

I'm already close, but he's taught me a lot about riding that edge. I've always done something similar when masturbating, but Bas has the pervy equivalent of advanced degrees in orgasm manipulation.

And I have been his eager student.

Once he's naked, he kneels between my legs and covers my body with his big, heavy warmth. His mouth covers my nipple and he sucks on it. The long, hard pulls combined with the low hum of the vibrator push me ever closer to the edge, but I want him inside me when I come.

"Bas, please."

He crawls a little farther up my body and the tip of his erection presses against my entrance.

He grips my jaw in his hand. Gentle but firm, and his expression is the same. "Ask me nicely. And make it filthy, little one."

I smile against his touch. "Please fuck me, Bas. Hold me down and take me hard."

"Perfect," he growls as he pushes the head in. And oh, that ache, immediately, because my bottom is still rudely taken up by that plug he loves so much. Before I can adjust, he snaps his hips forward until his entire length is buried deep inside my body. Another gasp, so good, before he's withdrawing and plunging in again.

Each thrust briefly presses the vibrator harder against my clit, then drives deeper against the plug, and I was a good girl. I got myself close.

So it doesn't take long for him to push me over the edge. As his rhythm picks up, my orgasm rips through me. And he's right behind me. Just as the final tremors subside and I turn to a puddle of happy goo, Bas finds his own release deep inside my body.

I'm vaguely aware of him moving away, then coming back, but it's not until he begins to unlace my boots that his voice penetrates my sex-drunk haze. "Come on, little one. I promised you a bath and it's ready and waiting for you."

When he's done undressing me, he lifts me into his arms and carries me to the bathroom. The last thing is a gentle removal of the plug, which he washes in the sink as I look around.

There's a bottle of red wine and two half-filled glasses on the small table next to the tub. This giant ensuite bathroom with a soaker for two was another brilliant modification Bas made when we combined the two apartments.

He climbs in first and I follow, settling between his legs and leaning against his chest while his thick cock presses into the small of my back.

He hands me a glass of wine, then picks up his own. His free hand lazily strokes up and down my front, occasionally cupping my breast or tweaking a nipple.

I may be used again tonight.

He might wring me out completely.

I smile and close my eyes. I'm such a lucky girl.

IF YOU ENJOYED THIS STORY, read Ellie and Gavin's story in *Prime Minister,* currently available! And coming soon, *Bull of the Woods,* Addison Greer's story. Turn the page for more about those books.

READ PRIME MINISTER NEXT!

Interested in reading more Frisky Beavers books, our sweet brand of kinky stories set in Ottawa? Start with Prime Minister!

Gavin:
Ellie Montague is smart, sensitive, and so gorgeous it hurts to look at her. She's also an intern in my office. The office of the Prime Minister of Canada.*
That's me. The PM.
She calls me that because when she calls me *Sir* I get hard and she gets flustered, and as long as she's my intern, I can't twist my hands in her strawberry-blonde hair and show her what else I'd like her to do with that pretty pink mouth.**

Ellie:
How much I like the PM varies on a daily basis. He's intense, controlling, and a perfectionist in every way—and he demands the same of his staff.
How much I want him never wavers.
There's something about him that tugs at me deep inside, and makes me wish that just once he'd cross the line in a late night

work session. I'd take that secret to the grave if it meant I got a taste of the barely restrained beast inside him.***

FOOTNOTES:
* This is a fictional erotic romance. No prime ministers or interns were harmed in the making of this book.
** Except it's a BDSM romance, so they were hurt a little.
*** Spoiler alert: she gets more than a taste. And she likes it.

GET IT HERE:
www.friskybeavers.com

COMING SOON: BULL OF THE WOODS

Jack:
The last person I expect to see in an Ottawa dungeon is Addison
Greer.
Mine.
She hasn't been that in four years, but I still remember how
perfect it was between us.

Addison:
They call him the Bull of the Woods, because he made his first
billion on lumber. Last I heard, he owned an NHL team in
Vancouver, which is the main reason I avoid the west coast.
So when Jack Benton strolls back into my life at the point I
finally decide to search for a new Master…
I'm not ready for him.
Not that I ever could be.
He was the only Dom to have my heart. And he broke it.

Jack:
I want a second chance.
And I always get what I want.

THE RULES:
* Itch-scratching only. No feelings allowed.
* No re-hashing the past.